C...

"The ... Bossa novas, bikinis, and bad ends
the h... or in this case, a Russian riverboat,
where murder is nothing to tap at. The cruise finds
them kick-ball-changing and flap-kicking their way
across Russia on a ship where murder points to
more than a few unusual suspects."
—**Nancy Coco**

"A fun read . . . the elements of hilarity and cama-
raderie between the characters make *Chorus Lines,
Caviar, and Corpses* intriguing and worth the read."
—**RT Book Reviews**

"A page-turning cozy mystery about five friends in
their fifties, dancing their way across Russia. From
the first chapter, McHugh delivers. . . . The cast of
characters includes endearing, scary, charming,
crazy, and irresistible people. Besides murder and
mayhem, we are treated to women who we might
want as our best friends, our shrinks, and our
travel companions."
—**Jerilyn Dufresne**

"Featuring travel tips and recipes, this series debut
features plenty of cozy adventure for armchair
travelers and mystery buffs alike. Sue Henry and
Peter Abresch fans will be delighted with this alternative."
—**Library Journal**

"Spasiba, Mary McHugh—that's Russian for 'thank you.' *Chorus Lines, Caviar, and Corpses* is a huge treat for armchair travelers and mystery fans alike, as five spirited tap dancers cruise from St. Petersburg to Moscow undeterred by a couple of shipboard murders. Vivid description and deft touches of local color take the reader right along with them."
—Peggy Ehrhart

"A fun book! Mary McHugh's *Chorus Lines, Caviar, and Corpses* is, quite literally, a romp. It has a little bit of everything, from tongue-in-cheek travel tips to romance and recipes (and oh, are they *good*). Not even the most jaded reader will be able to resist plucky Tina Powell and her cadre of capering cougars aboard a cruise ship where death is on the menu, along with the caviar. What could be more delicious?"
—Carole Bugge

"If you can't afford a Russian cruise up the Volga, this charming combination murder mystery travelogue, which mixes tasty cuisine and a group of frisky, wisecracking, middle-aged chorines, is the next best thing."
—Charles Salzberg

"I just finished *Chorus Lines, Caviar, and Corpses!* Oh, WOW, was it great! I read it in less than two days. So good! Thank you for writing this book, and I can't wait till the next one!"
—Shelley's Book Case

"I really enjoyed reading about the Happy Hoofers' trip on a Russian river cruise. This book had a lot

of action. I learned a lot about Russia that I never knew before. Great job, Mary. I look forward to the next installment in the Happy Hoofers Mystery Series."
—**Melina's Book Blog**

"I loved 'The Happy Hoofers' immediately. What a fun group. This mixes some of my favorite things in one book—a cruise ship setting, a group of friends, and a murder mystery. What could be better? This book moved along at a fast pace and had engaging characters—some nicer than others, of course. Add those things to a great setting and it's off on a wild adventure with a very interesting cast of characters."
—**Socrates' Book Review**

FLAMENCO, FLAN, AND FATALITIES

"*Flamenco, Flan, and Fatalities* serves up just what it says: good entertainment, good food, and good mystery! I am looking forward to reading other books in this series."
—**Back Porchervations**

"Talk about transporting the reader—I felt as if I were in Spain for the last few days."
—**Socrates Book Reviews**

"I enjoyed this book a little better than I did the first Happy Hoofer mystery. There were a lot of twists and turns in this book that kept me guessing."
—**Melina's Book Blog**

"This is a first-time read for me by this author and I adored her book . . . The characters are a hoot."
—**Bab's Book Bistro**

"I loved this book and reading about the great recipes included in the story. This book was full of adventure and mystery and had pulled me in and wouldn't let go!"
—**Community Bookstore**

Flamenco, Flan, and Fatalities is a lot of fun, a great read! I liked reading about the camaraderie of the five friends, and their sightseeing in Spain, just as much as trying to figure out *whodunit*. I really enjoyed it, and recommend *Flamenco, Flan, and Fatalities* to Cozy Mystery fans—armchair travelers, especially, will enjoy touring northern Spain on a luxury train with the Happy Hoofers."
—**Jane Reads**

"A very humorous mystery with a key emphasis on friendship. There is a bit of romance, and the recipes are great too. This can be read as a stand-alone, but I recommend starting at the beginning with *Chorus Lines, Caviar, and Corpses*. They are quick, entertaining reads and a great way to spend an afternoon."
—**Escape With Dollycas Into a Good Book**

Also by Mary McHugh

*Available from Kensington Publishing Corp.

Bossa Novas, Bikinis, and Bad Ends

Mary McHugh

KENSINGTON PUBLISHING CORP.
http://www.kensingtonbooks.com

KENSINGTON BOOKS are published by

Kensington Publishing Corp.
119 West 40th Street
New York, NY 10018

All Kensington Titles, Imprints, and Distributed Lines are available at special quantity discounts for bulk purchases for sales promotions, premiums, fund-raising, and educational or institutional use. Special book excerpts or customized printings can also be created to fit specific needs. For details, write or phone the office of the Kensington special sales manager: Kensington Publishing Corp., 119 West 40th Street, New York, NY 10018, attn: Special Sales Department, Phone: 1-800-221-2647.

Kensington and the K logo Reg. U.S. Pat & TM Off.

ISBN-13: 978-1-4967-0374-3
ISBN-10: 1-4967-0374-X
First Kensington Mass Market Edition: May 2016

eISBN-13: 978-1-4967-0375-0
eISBN-10: 1-4967-0375-8
First Kensington Electronic Edition: May 2016

10 9 8 7 6 5 4 3 2 1

Printed in the United States of America

*To Riva Nelson, who has been such a good friend
to me and an enthusiastic reader of my
Happy Hoofer series*

Chapter One

Welcome to Rio—Or Not

When I told my friends in New Jersey that the Happy Hoofers had been hired to dance at the Copacabana Palace, in Rio de Janeiro, they said, "It's a beautiful city." Then they would add, "But be careful. Hold on to your purse."

I was a little worried when we got on the plane in Newark, but I figured I was used to New York where I hang on to my handbag without even thinking about it, so I quashed my anxiety. I tend to worry too much about things anyway. I imagine all the bad things that can happen before I do anything and try to prevent them ahead of time. Of course, there's always something I couldn't have possibly foreseen. Like a murder or two, for instance.

I'm Pat Keeler, a family therapist, and I'm going to tell you the story of my adventure in Rio with my four best friends. We're a bunch of crazy, fiftyish in age, thirtyish-in-attitude tap dancers, known as the Happy Hoofers, and we were hired to perform at the luxurious Copacabana Palace. But our visit to Brazil turned out to be way different than any of us had expected. In fact, it was downright terrifying. We had been through some scary times in some of the other places where we danced, but this one beat them all.

Gini is always trying to get me to relax. "You just can't predict everything, Pat," she says in her usual exasperated way. "So you might as well relax."

Gini is great. She's my favorite of all my friends in this dancing troupe because she says what she thinks and is always honest with me. As a therapist, I'm used to people fooling themselves, trying to make me believe the illusions they foster about their relationships, so I cherish people who see life as it really is.

After we landed in Rio on a bright April afternoon, we loaded our bags and ourselves into a black limo provided by the hotel. The driver, whose bright smile more than made up for his fractured English, pointed out local attractions as he took us past a beautiful beach that stretched for twenty miles along the coast of the city.

We were staying at the Copacabana Palace Hotel on the Copacabana Beach. It really is a palace, pure white, and it seems to go on for acres. Built in the twenties, it was the place for movie stars and other celebrities to stay when they came to town. It was the only hotel for Marlene Dietrich, for instance, who, they told me, asked for a champagne bucket filled with sand in her dressing room because her dress was too tight to use the regular ladies' room. Ava Gardner trashed her room because she had just broken up with Frank Sinatra. Orson Welles threw furniture into the swimming pool after a fight with Dolores del Río. Even Edward, the temporary Prince of Wales, got drunk there and tried to catch fish in the fountain. It was a hotel for legends.

The manager, Miguel Ortega, greeted us at the front entrance. He was really good-looking, with black hair, dark, wicked-looking eyes, and a black beard and mustache surrounding a sensual mouth. He exuded a sexiness that was overpowering. He wore a charcoal-gray, expensive suit, and shoes that were definitely Prada.

"Welcome to the Copacabana, lovely ladies," he said with a slight but charming Portuguese accent. "We have been looking forward to your visit."

When Janice, our actress Hoofer, got out of the car, he ignored the rest of us and moved in on her like the ocean caressing the shore. "And you are?" he asked, taking her hand and kissing it. People always respond to Janice that way. She's used to it but can never understand what the fuss is about. She's so much more than just a beautiful face. She's won awards for her acting and directing, and she raised her daughter alone.

"I'm Janice Rogers, Senhor Ortega," she said, pushing her blond hair back from her face. "Your hotel is magnificent."

"As are you," he said, unable to take his eyes off her.

A woman who had been standing in back of Ortega stepped forward and put her arm through his. "We are so glad to have you here this week," she said to us. "I'm Maria Oliveira and will be your translator and guide while you're here. I will show you Rio, and I hope you will allow me to help you with anything you need." She was a slender woman, in her early thirties, her hair in tight braids all over her head, her skin a pale brown. Her English was flawless, with no trace of an accent.

She gently pulled Miguel away from Janice and asked, "Which one of you is Tina Powell?"

Tina, a magazine editor and our fearless leader, held out her hand. "I'm Tina," she said. "We are grateful to have your help, Maria. None of us knows Portuguese, so we will rely on you."

Miguel tore his gaze from Janice to Tina and kissed her hand. "We will do everything we can to make your stay here a pleasant one," he said.

"I'm sure you will," Tina said. "Thank you, Senhor Ortega."

She introduced him to Gini, a documentary filmmaker, Mary Louise, our housewife Hoofer, and me. He guided our group into the imposing lobby of this incredible hotel. Everything about it was grand. The lobby was huge, and the marble floors and columns gleamed in the afternoon sunshine. The Happy Hoofers were definitely moving up in the world.

"After you get unpacked and rested and have some dinner," Maria said, "I'd like to take you to one of my favorite places in Rio. I don't want to tell you much about it because I want it to be a surprise. It's a typically Brazilian experience."

"Sounds intriguing," Tina said. "We're looking forward to it. See you later, Maria."

We got our keys at the desk and went up to our rooms.

When I saw the suite I would share with Gini, I was impressed. It had a huge sitting room with a balcony that had a view of the beach, an iPod dock, a wide-screen TV, a fully stocked minibar, and WiFi. There was a sleek modern bedroom with abstract paintings on the walls, an enormous marble-tiled bathroom with a bidet, a separate shower and bathtub, and a little kitchen with an espresso machine. Gini and I grinned at each other when we saw our home for the next week. "Sure beats New Jersey," Gini said.

"Oh, yeah!" I said. "Look at that beach. It's huge. You could fit the whole Jersey shore on that sand."

Gini went out on the balcony. "I know," she said. "Acres of sand and water just waiting for us to dive in. Want to go for a swim?"

"Do you think it's safe?" I said, worrywart that I am. I try not to be one, but it's no use. I was born that way.

"Unless there's a demon undertow waiting to drag us out to sea, never to be heard from again, I think we're fine," Gini said, throwing one of the ten silk-encased pillows on her bed at me.

"I'll go ask the others if they want to come with us," she said and left the room. "Don't go without me."

I unpacked and put my clothes in the drawers and closet. By the time Gini got back into the room, I had slithered into my two-piece, black bathing suit that, I have to say, really showed off my dancer-slim, flat-stomached, terrific-legged, figure. Tap dancing will do that.

"Way to go, Pat," Gini said. "That bikini is perfect for you."

"Come on, Gini," I said, embarrassed. "You're the one with the big boobs. Are Jan and Mary Louise and Tina coming to the beach with us?"

"No, they wanted to finish unpacking and shower. Maybe rest up for a while."

"They don't have your energy, Gini," I said. "But then, who does?"

"Too little time, too much to do," she said, putting on her own swimsuit, which proved my point. "I want a swim first."

We threw shirts over our suits and grabbed some sunblock, dark glasses, and towels and headed for the elevator.

As we walked out onto the beach, which was crowded with sun worshipers, we felt overdressed. Others on the beach wore string bikinis and thongs so tiny, our swimsuits felt like granny gowns by comparison. Topless bathing was not allowed on the beaches in Rio, but the tops the women wore were practically nonexistent. They left very little to the imagination. The sun blazed down on us. It felt like it was about ninety degrees, so the thought of the cooling ocean was enticing. The sand was gleaming white and clean. Cleaner than any of the beaches I've seen at home. We dropped our stuff near the water's edge and ran into the sea.

The tide was going out, so we had to push our way through the shallow waves for a short distance before it was deep enough to swim. The water was cool, not icy cold the way it is on Cape Cod, where my family took me as a child and is still my favorite place to vacation. I dove in and swam out to deeper water, taking long strokes, not having to kick my legs very hard because the sea pushed me along. It felt glorious.

Gini caught up with me before long. Her style was shorter strokes and faster leg movements, just like her personal style on shore. We swam along together side by side in the salty water, looking up occasionally long enough to smile at each other.

Gini turned over on her back and kicked her legs. "Is this great or what?" she said.

I rolled over onto my back, too, and did a slow, lazy backstroke.

"How did we get so lucky, Gini?" I asked. "We're in Rio de Janeiro, Brazil! Getting paid to sleep in a gorgeous suite, and swimming off one of the best beaches in the world. We must be doing something right."

"Maybe God likes dancers," she said. "Maybe He wishes there were more of us, so He does things like this to encourage others to take up dancing too."

I'm not always sure there's a God up there helping us along, but I felt too blessed to argue with her.

"Race you back to shore," I said, flipping over and swimming toward the beach.

We kept even until the very last lap, when Gini passed me with a burst of energy, ran up on the sand, and flopped down on her towel. A trio of tanned teenagers interrupted their volleyball game long enough to admire her.

I shook myself when I came out of the water and spattered droplets all over my competitive friend. "You always have to win, don't you?" I asked.

"Second best is no good," she said, drying her red hair. "At least, it's not as much fun."

"You should know," I said. "You're definitely a winner, Gini. I wish I were more like you."

She made a face and said, "Watch what you wish for, Pat. But I keep trying."

"Let's just lie here and not try to do anything," I said.

"As if you could," Gini said.

"Watch me," I said.

I lay back on my towel to soak in that life-restoring sun when a man and a woman stopped in front of us, casting a shadow.

"Are you two with the Happy Hoofers?" the man asked.

I squinted and shaded my eyes as I looked up at him. He was dark-skinned, sexy-looking, with a gorgeous body. So many good-looking men in this city. It was almost enough to turn me into a heterosexual. Almost.

The woman with him was wearing a barely visible top and a thong. Her large sunglasses covered most of her face and made it hard for me to get an accurate idea of what she looked like, but her lips were sensual and shiny.

Gini spoke first—of course. "We are. Who wants to know?"

The man held out his hand. "I am Lucas. I used to be the bartender at the hotel. This is Yasmin. She still works at the hotel—as an accountant."

Yasmin looked at us over the top of her Ray-Bans and said, "Actually, I'm the only accountant. I'm glad to meet you." She didn't really look all that glad.

"What can we do for you?" Gini said. Her manner was not friendly. I was surprised because Gini is usually open to all comers.

"Nothing," Lucas said, sensing her hostility and starting to move away. "I just thought I'd introduce myself to you in case you wanted to see the sights in Rio. I work as a guide now."

"Thanks," Gini said. "I don't think so. Maria has planned our schedule while we're here."

At the mention of Maria's name, Lucas's smile vanished, and his eyes narrowed. He grabbed Yasmin's arm and pulled her away. "Enjoy your visit," he muttered, clearly not meaning it.

When they were out of earshot, I said to Gini,

"What was that all about? You weren't your usual warm and kindly self with them."

"I don't know what it was about those two," Gini said, sitting up. "There was just something about them I didn't like. Did you see his face when I mentioned Maria's name?"

"Yeah," I said. "I wondered about that. He definitely doesn't like her."

"I'll see what I can find out why when we meet Maria later for our mysterious trip," Gini said.

"You'll be too busy taking pictures to ask her anything, if I know you," I said. Gini was a professional photographer. She truly loved taking pictures. She took photos and videos wherever we went. I was always amazed at how unusual her shots were. She was brilliant at finding a different angle, a different perspective, a fresh new way of looking at things. I guess that's why she wins prizes with her documentaries.

"Well, I'll try to find out about those two between shots," Gini said.

I picked up my towel and lotion. "Let's go back," I said, putting on my shirt.

We took showers and dressed for dinner in silk pantsuits.

We met our gang and Maria in the lobby. It was even more elegant at night, with the chandeliers glowing and only one person behind the main desk.

"Please be our guests for dinner in the Palm Room," Maria said, gesturing toward a restaurant that was lush with greenery. "Afterward, as promised, I'll take you to a side of Rio that very few tourists ever experience."

"Sounds exciting," Gini said.

"Meet me here at seven," Maria said. "Wear comfortable shoes. And be sure to bring your sense of adventure."

Pat's Tip for Traveling with Friends: Always bring earplugs, in case your roommate snores.

Chapter Two

Magical Mystery Tour

At dinner in the quiet, softly lit, luxurious dining room, with its tables set far enough apart so that guests could talk without being overheard, we feasted on partridge with acerola fruit sauce—divine!

"What's in this sauce?" Mary Louise asked the waiter. "What's acerola?"

"Oh, senhora, it's a berry."

"What kind of berry? I've never tasted anything like it before."

"It tastes like a combination of apple and cherry," he said. "I don't think you have it in the States. It's found mostly in Central and South America. It's especially good with partridge, I think."

"It's marvelous," Mary Louise said. "Thank you."

The waiter was pleased. He loved answering questions about the food he served, and he especially enjoyed answering Mary Louise's queries. She so obviously loved food and cooking.

"I'll certainly miss this food when we get home," Mary Louise said. "Back to roast chicken and baked potatoes."

"Your cooking is wonderful," Tina said. "You're way beyond roast chicken."

After dinner, we met Maria in the lobby. She looked stunning in a white pants suit and turquoise earrings. She led us outside the hotel to a white van with the hotel logo painted on its sides. We drove through the main streets of Rio. As we wove through the traffic, we saw a beautiful, modern city. People in bright summer clothing strolled the busy streets, vendors hawked their wares from sidewalk stands, and high above the city on Corcovado Mountain stood the statue of Christ the Redeemer, His arms spread in a timeless, benevolent gesture. After about fifteen minutes our driver turned onto a narrow dark street paved with cobblestones and stopped in front of a rather seedy little house. Its chipped paint and dusty windows contrasted with the gleaming glass-and-steel structures closer to the beach.

Maria led us into the building and down some stairs to a large basement room. On the stone floor, a half-dozen women dressed in white robes were dancing barefoot, swaying, their eyes closed, as a muscular, dark-skinned man provided a hypnotic rhythm on a colorfully decorated drum. Mesmerized, we sat on wicker chairs to observe the scene.

As we watched, one of the women went into a trance. She stood out from the other women in the room because her head was clean-shaven. Her face was thin, her cheekbones prominent. I could not stop looking at her. The room was still as her body shook and she fell to the floor. For a while she was motionless. Then she rose up, lit a cigar, opened her eyes, and beckoned to Maria.

Maria walked toward her as if she were hypnotized, as if she had no choice.

"Your name is Maria?" the psychic asked.

"It is," she said, her voice a monotone.

"You are in great danger. Someone wants to kill you."

"Who?" Maria asked.

"I do not know. But I feel the presence of evil around you."

"You have to tell me who wants to kill me," Maria said, panic in her voice.

The mystic handed her cigar to another woman nearby, closed her eyes, and fell to the floor again. She swayed back and forth, then opened her eyes and looked at Maria.

"You have taken something that belongs to this person. If you don't give it back, you will be killed."

"You have to tell me more about whoever it is who wants to harm me," Maria said, shaking the mystic's arm.

The woman slumped over, her head in her lap, and was silent, unreachable.

Maria returned to our group, shaken. Mary Louise, our mother hen, pulled a chair over for her to sit on and knelt beside her.

"You can't believe anything she said. She doesn't know you, Maria. She's just making all that stuff up. It's her job to be dramatic like that."

Maria shook her head. "These people have special powers. They can see things nobody else can. I believe her. She knew my name. There was no way she could have known my name." She looked around at the rest of us, fear in her eyes.

"I'm so sorry," she said. "I brought you here because I thought it would be different from anything you would see at home, but I didn't mean for it to turn out like this." She gave a short laugh.

I wasn't sure I wanted to hear anything one of these mystics would tell me, but I could see that Gini was practically bursting to interact with them. As a documentary filmmaker, she's always looking for new subjects to explore. She had already made a prize-winning film about Hurricane Katrina in New Orleans, and I could tell she sniffed another unusual experience in this cellar in Rio.

Tina got Maria a glass of water. "Are you all right?" she asked.

"I will be," she said, but she didn't look at all sure of that.

Janice, who was always up for anything, obviously wanted to be beckoned by one of the women in white. She tried waving at one of them, but nothing happened. They ignored her. That was probably the first time that ever happened to Jan.

The drumbeat began again, softly at first, then louder and stronger, rhythmically, hypnotically, and the women in white moved their bodies back and forth, their arms reaching up, their eyes closed, their heads turning from side to side. My own body began to sway. I couldn't help it.

A tall woman in the center opened her eyes wide and motioned to Gini. "Come," she said in Portuguese. Gini grabbed Maria and dragged her to the middle of the floor in front of the mystic. Maria obviously didn't want to go back there, but as our translator, she was forced to follow Gini.

"I see you in India," the woman said. Gini gasped. She had just returned from India with her boyfriend, Alex, attempting to adopt a little girl she had met while filming a documentary on orphanages in New Delhi. There was no way this woman could possibly have known that. Gini leaned forward to hear the mystic's next words.

"You left something there that is very precious to you," the psychic said, covering her eyes with long bony fingers. "You must go back and get it."

"Will I be able to do that?" Gini asked through Maria.

"It will be more difficult than you are anticipating, but you will be successful eventually. You must keep going back there until your wish is granted." The woman turned away from Gini and her eyes widened when she looked at Maria.

"You . . ." she said. "You . . ." and she fell to the floor.

Gini put her arm around Maria and led her back to us. "Don't pay any attention to her," she said.

"You paid attention to what she told you, didn't you?" Maria demanded.

"Well, of course. I want to believe her, but I—"

Maria grabbed Gini by the shoulders. "How did she know you were in India?"

"Oh, they probably have hidden microphones around the room, and they heard me talking about it before," Gini said.

I knew Gini hadn't been talking about her little girl in the Indian orphanage this evening, but I kept my mouth shut. I must say, though, I was curious. How did the so-called mystic know this? I mean with all the places in the world she could have mentioned, why did she pick India? Listen, I don't believe in all this mystical stuff, but I had to admit that there are things that happen all the time that we can't understand. I try not to let that sneak into my therapy, but it's not always easy. There often seems to be some other force at work that I can't explain.

Janice didn't wait to be summoned. She walked up to the nearest psychic, whose face was gaunt and pale, and put her hands together in a pleading way. Her face is so beautiful, it's hard for people to resist anything she asks. Her perfect complexion and her velvety blue eyes are very hard to resist. She never consciously uses her beauty to get what she wants, but almost everyone responds to her. Must be nice.

The psychic stared at Janice and said something to her in Portuguese. Janice realized she needed Maria and beckoned to her. Janice pointed to the translator and the woman repeated what she had said.

"What did she say, Maria?" Janice asked.

"She asked if you would have a drink with her," Maria said, trying not to laugh.

I was close enough to hear this exchange, and I did laugh. Who would have expected that?

I should explain that I live with a woman I love very much—her name is Denise. I have always been attracted to women, though I tried to deny it for a long time. When I finally accepted this truth about myself, I found peace. Denise and I have been happy together since we met on a train in Spain the Happy Hoofers were hired to dance on. Her son, David, lives with us, and I couldn't love him more if he were my own son. He's a sensitive, loving, brilliant boy who brings so much joy into my life.

The whole idea that this mysterious, mystical, eerie experience should turn into an invitation for a drink from a mystic attracted to Janice delighted me.

Janice looked startled at first, and then she smiled.

"Maria," she said, "please thank her for me and tell her I'm busy tonight."

Maria repeated the message in Portuguese.

The woman looked disappointed, but she put her hands on Janice's face and said in English, "Beautiful. You will always be lucky."

Janice smiled and touched the woman's face, "*Obrigada,* senhora." That was one of the few Portuguese words I knew. It meant "Thank you."

None of us wanted to leave, but Maria gathered us up and led us back up the stairs and into the van waiting to take us back to the hotel. I could tell she was still shaken by what the psychic had said to her, but she did her best to pretend she wasn't.

"So what did you think?" she asked us. "Were you convinced that those women had magical powers?

"Well, I'd sure like to know how she knew about Amalia in India," Gini said. "That was spooky. But I wouldn't have missed it for anything. Thanks for taking us there, Maria."

"You're welcome, my doubting one," Maria said. "I sincerely hope she was wrong about someone wanting to kill me." She shivered involuntarily.

"Of course she was," Gini said. "Why would anyone want to kill you?"

Maria didn't say anything for a minute. "Well . . ." She looked as if she wanted to say more, but she shook her head and said, "I can't imagine."

Why didn't I believe her?

We arrived at the hotel. Maria walked with us to the elevator and said, "Meet me in the Piano

Bar for a drink in an hour. It's beautiful late at night, and I'd love to know all of you better."

We went back to our rooms to unwind a bit.

"Did you believe those mystics, Gini?" I asked.

"Well, I have to admit, she blew my mind when she brought up India, Pat. How on earth could she know about that? I said there must have been hidden mikes in that room, and maybe there were, but I don't remember talking about Amalia and the orphanage while we were there. Did I?"

"I'm pretty sure you didn't," I said. "That surprised me too. But you seemed so calm about it."

"I just didn't want to show how shaken I was," she said.

"Well, let's hope she was wrong about someone planning to kill Maria. I'd like to get through this week without anybody being murdered."

Gini nodded. "It certainly seems to happen a lot when we show up," she said.

"Are you ready?" I asked. "Let's go downstairs."

We went down to the bar, which lived up to Maria's description. Long and gleaming, with comfortable stools and elegant little tables near a grand piano where a man played soft, soothing music, it was the perfect place to relax and talk about our first day in Rio. We sat down at a table near the piano, where our friends had already gathered.

"I'm so glad we have Maria as our guide," Tina said. She was wearing a pale blue silky top and pants that made her blue eyes even more beautiful than usual. "She obviously knows Rio well and can take us to places like that weird house with those women in white. That was great—except for the part about someone planning to kill her, of course. That was spooky."

"I loved it," Janice said, her blond hair swept back off her bare shoulders, "but I had the feeling that Maria doesn't like me all that much. I don't know why."

"She probably thought you were trying to steal her boyfriend—the hotel manager, Miguel," Gini said. "He zeroed in on you right away. I saw the look on Maria's face when he couldn't take his eyes off you."

"Oh, come on, Gini," Janice said. "He was just being polite."

"Yeah, right," Gini said, "Miss I'm-Nothing-Special. All men react to you like that. I hope you know it's the only reason we keep you in our group. We get more applause with you there."

Janice dribbled some of her margarita on Gini's hair.

"Wonder where Maria is," Mary Louise said. "It's been an hour and a half since we left her. That's not like her. She was right on time this afternoon."

"We should call her room," I said. "Maybe she got involved in something and can't get away." I pulled out my phone and asked the man at the desk to dial Maria's room. There was no answer.

"She'll turn up," Janice said. "It's so lovely here. I don't mind waiting."

We were listening to the music and enjoying the quiet of the late evening when the door of the hotel burst open and the lobby was filled with uniformed police. Miguel hurried by our table. Tina stopped him as he went by.

"Miguel, what's happening?"

"It's Maria," he said, pausing for a moment. "She's . . ."

"Tell us," Tina said. "We were waiting for her. Is she all right?"

"She's . . ." he stammered. "There's been a . . . She's dead."

Pat's Tip for Traveling with Friends: Make sure one of you knows a few words in the language of the country you're in.

Chapter Three

What's Another Murder Among Friends?

Gini jumped up, knocking over her chair. "What do you mean she's dead?" she asked. "We just saw her a couple of hours ago. How could she be dead? What happened to her?"

"I don't know," Miguel said. "I have to talk to the police." He hurried to the lobby.

The police officers surrounded Miguel, who was talking rapidly to the one who seemed to be in charge. Miguel pointed to us, and the man he had been talking to headed toward our table, led by Miguel.

"Sit down, Gini," Tina said in a low voice. "Cool it, everybody."

Miguel spoke first. "Forgive this intrusion, ladies," he said. "There has been an unfortunate occurrence in our hotel. One of our employees—Maria, your translator—has been found dead in her room, and Senhor Pereira, chief of police here in Rio, would like to ask you a few questions, if you don't mind."

"Of course we don't mind, Senhor Ortega," Tina said. "We'd be glad to help in any way we can."

The police chief, who was about our age, with dark hair starting to gray at the temples, observant brown eyes, and a slim, muscular body, bowed and said, "I understand you were with Senhora Oliveira this evening. I thought perhaps you could give me some information about her—anything that seemed suspicious to you or could shed some light on her death."

We all looked toward Tina, our official spokesperson, the most articulate of our group. Even Gini waited for her to answer the officer.

"We would be glad to tell you anything that would be helpful, Senhor Pereira," Tina said. "Maria was our guide and translator and she took us to a—a—I don't really know what to call it. It was a house with women—psychics, Maria said—who told us our future—and—" She paused, not sure how to proceed.

"One of the women told Maria someone wanted to kill her," Gini said, leaping right in, the way she always does.

The police chief's attention turned to Gini. "And you are?"

"Oh, excuse me, senhor," she said. "I'm Gini Miller. I didn't mean to interrupt, but it was so startling to hear the psychic—or whatever she was—say that. She told Maria that she had taken something from the person who wanted to kill her and that she had to give it back or she would die."

"How did Senhora Oliveira react to this?" Captain Pereira asked.

"Like you'd expect her to," Gini said, impatiently. "She was terrified. She believed this woman."

"Do you remember the name of the psychic who told her this?"

"No," Gini said. "Nobody told us any of their names, but she was the only woman there whose head was shaven. She was amazing looking."

"Did Senhora Oliveira give you any idea of who this person might be who wanted to kill her?" the police chief asked.

"No, she was shaking all over. I got the feeling that she knew what the woman meant, but she wouldn't tell us. How did Maria die? Did someone kill her?"

"We won't know until the medical examiner finishes with her."

"I mean, was she shot or stabbed or something?" Gini asked. She has the soul of a journalist. She always needs to know all the details of the circumstances she finds herself in. I find out more stuff just hanging out with her.

"I can't tell you any more right now," Pereira

said. "Any information about Senhora Oliveira's death has to be confidential at the moment. I'm sure you understand."

"Of course," Gini said, but I knew she still had a million questions. She would never give up.

The police chief looked around the table at the rest of us. His eyes lingered on Janice's face the longest, of course. How could he help it?

"Did any of you notice anything that might be helpful to us?" he asked.

"It seemed like she knew who would try to kill her," Tina said. "That's just a feeling I had. Nothing she told us about. She started to say something in the car coming back to the hotel, but she stopped. She just met us this afternoon, so she didn't really know us. I'm sure she wasn't going to reveal any secrets about her life."

"Thank you for your help," Pereira said. He turned to Miguel.

"Would you please assemble your staff in your office, Senhor Ortega," he said. "I would like to ask them some questions."

"Of course," Miguel said. "If possible, senhor, I would like to keep the guests of the hotel out of this as much as possible." He pulled out his phone to call his people.

"I cannot promise you anything, Senhor Ortega," Pereira said. "At this point everyone is a suspect, including your guests."

"I understand," Miguel said.

The police chief went into the lobby to instruct his officers.

While Miguel was talking on the phone to assemble his staff, a stunning woman a little younger than we were got out of the elevator and ran up to Miguel. She had blond hair, which I'm sure started off life a lot darker than it was now. Her skin was pale olive, smooth, and wrinkle-free. Her eyes were dark with long lashes, definitely Asian. Her figure was slim with small breasts, almost nonexistent hips, and long legs. She wore a white silk dress with a mandarin collar. She looked annoyed.

"What is happening, Miguel?" she said. "I couldn't sleep with all this noise. What's going on?"

Miguel, equally irritated when he saw her, snapped at her, "There's been a death, Sumiko," he said. "Maria is dead. Go back to bed. There's nothing you can do here."

"Dead?" she said. "What do you mean 'dead'? Maria was too young to die. What happened to her? Did someone kill her? Tell me, Miguel. I'm not a child. I'm not going back to bed. I need to know what is going on here." She snatched the phone out of his hand and held it behind her back.

Miguel grabbed her roughly and tore the phone out of her hand. "I'll tell you all about it later, Sumiko," he said. "This is not the time to argue with me. I want you to leave me alone." His voice was low and angry.

"I'm not going anywhere, Miguel," she said, pulling away from him.

"Nice loving couple," Gini said to me out of the corner of her mouth.

"Do you think that's his wife?" I whispered back to her.

"Well, if she is, they have a very unfriendly relationship," Gini said.

Miguel noticed us talking to each other and reverted to his hotel manager's expression and voice.

"May I present my wife, Sumiko?" he said. "Sumiko, these are the Happy Hoofers, the dancers I told you about who are going to perform for us." He introduced each one of us by name.

Sumiko glanced at us briefly, unsmiling.

"How many of them are you planning to sleep with, Miguel?" she said. "That blonde first?" She pointed to Janice.

I grabbed Gini's arm before she could punch this unpleasant woman.

Without waiting for an answer, Sumiko turned and walked into the lobby to speak to the chief of police.

"She's upset by all the turmoil," Miguel said apologetically. "She's not usually this rude. Please excuse her." His frown said he did not forgive her. He moved a short distance away and continued to make calls on his phone.

We leaned in closer to each other so we could talk without his hearing us.

"Well, this is another fine mess you've gotten us into, Tina," Gini said, and we all stifled our laughter.

"Yeah, Tina," Mary Louise said, teasing her.

"Can't you get us a job where everyone stays alive until we go home?"

"You're a rotten bunch," Tina said, laughing in spite of herself. "Next time I'll make sure one of you gets it."

"I think it should be Gini," Janice said. "She's the biggest troublemaker in our group."

"Definitely Gini," I said, ratting out my best friend. "She probably killed Maria so we could be mentioned in *The New York Times* again."

"Well, you have to admit, it would be a great story for Alex," Gini said. Alex Boyer is her boyfriend who used to be the bureau chief in Moscow for the *Times*. She met him when we danced on our Moscow to St. Petersburg cruise. They fell in love, and he transferred back to the *Times*'s New York office so he could be near her. He's a fantastic guy. Very smart, loving, kind. He'd do anything for Gini. They're planning to marry one of these days, but right now, they are having a great time together. He wants to help her adopt the little girl in the orphanage in India.

We all love Alex because he loves Gini so much. Gini was married before but divorced her husband because he wanted her to stay home and clean the house instead of making prize-winning films and traveling around the world. His idea of an exciting time was watching football on the couch with beer and potato chips.

"I think Alex would be a little annoyed to have to visit you in jail all the time," Tina said. "But come back to the here and now, Hoofers.

Do we stay here and dance as if nothing has happened or give up our fee and go back home? I need a vote."

"For heaven's sake, let's go back home," I said. "I'm sick of people getting murdered all the time. Every time we dance somewhere, someone turns up dead. I want to go back to good old New Jersey where people die of old age." I know. I was being my safe, unexciting, boring self, but therapists are supposed to be sensible.

"Are you nuts?" Gini said. "Come on, Pat. We can't go home until we find out what she died of. We're all assuming someone killed her because of what that psychic said, but maybe she just died of a heart attack. We don't know anything, really. We might as well dance. That's what we do."

"Do you really believe she died of a heart attack, Gini?" I said. "A healthy, active, relatively young person who obviously had nothing wrong with her when she took us to that house. I don't think so."

"Probably not," Gini said. "But don't you want to stick around until we find out what happened to her?"

"Yeah, Pat," Janice said. "Anyway, aside from the murder, you don't want to leave Rio until we've been to the top of Sugar Loaf Mountain, do you? All we've seen so far is a bunch of strange ladies dancing and falling on the floor."

"Listen, Pat," Mary Louise said, "it took me a week to persuade George that I could go to Rio and not get killed. We have to stay. Please say yes, oh wise one." She put her hands together in a prayerful pose.

I can never resist Mary Louise. She's so sweet and dear. I'm always glad she gets a chance to get away from George once in a while. He's such a . . . such a . . . man!

"Oh, all right, you bloodthirsty Hoofers," I said. "But next time we go someplace where everybody lives to be a hundred and two."

"Oh, that'll be easy to find!" Gini said.

"Then we're agreed?" Tina said. "We stay and dance for our supper? Speak now or forever hold your peace."

Everybody, including me, nodded yes.

"We're the Happy Hoofers," Mary Louise said. "We dance through anything."

"Pat," Tina said. "You're sure?"

"I'm sure, Tina," I said, not at all sure of anything.

Tina got permission from the police chief for us to go back to our rooms and get some sleep, with the understanding that we would be available to answer more questions the next day. Tina asked Miguel who would replace Maria as our translator and guide.

"I've asked Natalia, one of our entertainers, to show you our city," Miguel said. "She speaks perfect English and knows this city backward and forward. She said she would be delighted to be your guide."

"Thank you, Miguel," Tina said, herding us all into the elevator and off to a good night's sleep.

Pat's Tip for Traveling with Friends: It's faster to ask directions from a native of the country than to wait for someone to find them on her smart phone.

Chapter Four

Thank You, God

After a quick breakfast the next morning, we were scooped up by an effervescent, totally ditzy marvel of a woman named Natalia, who twinkled up to us, bright and lethally cheerful at that hour of the day.

"My little Hoofers!" she exclaimed, shaking hands with each one of us, then giving us a quick hug and a kiss on the cheek. To tell you the truth, I'm a little put off by this much familiarity so soon after meeting someone, but I squashed my unfriendly feelings and welcomed this flibberti-gibbet of a woman with the rest of my friends.

"I am Natalia!" she said. She seemed to talk

only in exclamation points. She was a tiny little person with reddish blond hair swept up on top of her head, a face made up to startle the sun, and silver and onyx earrings that almost reached her shoulders. She was wearing a turquoise blouse with very tight white leggings and stiletto heels that no one else could possibly walk in, but she seemed to dance in place in them. I had my doubts about how good a guide she would be.

"You would like to see the Christ on top of Corcovado Mountain?" she asked. Without waiting for an answer, she fluttered us all out to a waiting van and climbed into the front seat next to a man she introduced as Ramon. He was a sturdy, trusty-looking man who smiled at us and said, "Welcome to Rio, senhoras."

"*Vamanos,* Ramon!" she said patting his arm. "To Corcovado!"

Then she turned to face us in the back of the van. "You will love our city," she said. "It is so beautiful." She paused. "Just don't go out by yourself at night."

"Why not?" Gini asked. "Is there a lot of crime in Rio?"

Natalia made a face. "Not exactly a lot," she said. "But not exactly a little either."

"We don't have to leave the hotel to find it, evidently," Gini said. "Did you hear about Maria? She might have been murdered. Nobody has admitted that yet, but . . ."

Natalia looked down at her blouse and flicked at something on the front.

"Um—yes," she said. "I did hear about Maria.

That's why I'm with you today instead of her. She's—uh—you know—dead." She examined her fingernails and sighed. "Terrible thing."

"Why would anyone want to kill her?" Gini asked. You can see why I love this woman. She always asks the questions everyone else is thinking but doesn't have the nerve to express.

"Turn left up here, Ramon," Natalia said, squirming in her seat to look out the front window.

"Natalia?" Gini said.

"Let's not talk about that just now," Natalia said. "We are going to take the train up to the top of the mountain and when you see that one hundred and twenty-five-foot statue of Christ, you will marvel."

She started talking faster and faster." Did you know that one time a man—his name was Felix Baumgartner—from Austria—climbed up to one of the Savior's hands on ropes and parachuted off it to the ground? Ninety-five feet! We couldn't get over it. It was such an outrageous thing to do. People said it was sacrilegious. Every time I go up there I just am so amazed that anyone would try a stunt like that. Imagine! He jumped right off. Turn at the next corner, Ramon. No, not there. The next one." She kept babbling on, waving her perfectly manicured hands around, poking at her hair, straightening her blouse.

Gini nudged me and twirled her finger around near her head. She mouthed, "What a ditz."

Tina, our always gracious Tina, said, "We're really looking forward to this, Natalia. I've heard about it all my life—how moving an experience it is. We appreciate your making the time to take us there."

Natalia almost fell over the back of the seat with relief. "It is my pleasure!" she said.

Ramon pulled up in front of the entrance. Natalia bought tickets and ushered us all aboard the red and white, two-car train that would take us to the top of the mountain. As we rode up the steep trail through a thick forest, we occasionally saw some intrepid hikers climbing up the path that ran alongside the tracks. I could not imagine making this seventeen-minute train trip on foot in this heat. Gini was busy taking pictures of the city of Rio spread beneath us. The rest of us were listening to Natalia give a brief history of this mountain and the statue at the top.

"Corcovado Mountain is 2330 feet high," she said, "and its name means 'hunchback' because of its shape—like a cone. Long before the statue of Christ was erected on this mountain, Emperor Pedro II loved riding a donkey to the top of it. He decided to build a railroad track with steam trains that would take other people up there to enjoy the view, without having to ride a mule. The statue of Christ was created in France by a sculptor named Paul Landowski, who shipped it in parts to Rio, where it was assembled in 1931. Just the head alone weighs thirty tons and each of the arms weighs eighty tons. It was an amazing feat."

When we got off the train, that first sight of Christ towering above us, His arms outstretched to embrace all of us sinners below, was overpowering. I'm not that religious. I went to Sunday school sporadically when I was a little girl, but I haven't been to church in years. I'm sort of a Presbyterian, but I couldn't tell you the difference between that denomination and all the other Protestant faiths. I just have this love of Christ and His teaching of peace, love one another, look out for each other, help the poor and sick, do unto others as you would have them do unto you, that has stayed with me all these years. I try to practice what He preached, but I fall far short.

Sort of instinctively, each of us Hoofers went off by herself to a corner of the plaza to look up at that enormous white granite statue with Christ's face blessing us from above. I felt that He was looking at me, that His spirit reached down into my heart and gave me a feeling of peace and quiet and warmth that I don't often have in this clackety world we live in.

All my questions and worries and anxieties about the dance we would do that night, about Maria's death, about Denise back home without me, about my wanting a drink sometimes, just went away, disappeared. I was alone on that mountaintop with Christ. I could feel His arms around me, hear Him reassure me that I was safe, that nothing bad was going to happen to me because He was looking after me.

All the other people in the crowd around me seemed invisible. They were quiet too. Part of it was the overwhelming size of this huge sculpture. Part of it was being so high up above all the problems and little anxieties down below. I had never felt like this before. I once climbed to the top of the Statue of Liberty and felt a surge of love for our country, but it was nothing like this feeling of surrender to a force much stronger than I.

I looked up once at the same time Mary Louise did, and there were tears in both our eyes. She smiled at me, and I smiled back. Both of us knew exactly what the other was thinking. *Thank you, God. We have so much.*

After a few minutes of this totally peaceful experience, I was aware of a fluttery little red-headed being flitting among us to take us back to the train.

"Come along," she said, her hand on my arm, pulling me toward the platform where the train was waiting to take us back to the city below. I said another "Thank you" silently and followed her.

"That was unbelievable, Natalia," Mary Louise said. "Thank you for taking us up there. I'll never forget it."

We all murmured our own expressions of gratitude for this unforgettable experience.

When we piled out of the train and were herded back into the van, Natalia bubbled into the front seat again and said to Ramon, "To the Samba." Then she leaned over the front seat, waving her hands, talking fast.

"I am taking you to my favorite restaurant for lunch," she said. "It's called the Samba because they play samba music all the time, and because the food is divine. Wait till you taste it. Very Brazilian. I thought you would want the full Rio experience!"

"That's perfect, Natalia," Tina said. "We're dancing the samba tonight at the hotel."

"I know, I know," Natalia said, practically falling into Tina's lap. "I am going to sing while you dance. You dance to the song 'Copacabana,' no?"

"Yes, that's right," Tina said. "Should be good. Actually, I'd like to get back to the hotel and re-hearse with you."

"Good idea," Natalia said. "But let's eat first."

We stopped in front of a small restaurant, and Natalia flitterered and fluttered us in the door the way she always does. She never seemed to stop moving—back and forth, around and around, until we were all seated at a table near the window. There was nothing particularly Brazilian about the room. We could have been in New York. The tables were set close together and there were no cloths on them. Then the music started. It was a samba so compelling, I wanted to get up and dance to it. All of us were moving our shoulders and torsos in time to the strong beat of the song. Natalia was obviously delighted to see us caught up in the mood and the rhythm of the music.

"I think you will be part Brazilian when you go back to the United States," she said. "Our music has become a part of you."

"You're right, Natalia," Tina said. "It's impossible to sit still."

"I can sit still long enough to eat," Gini said. "What should we order, Natalia? We don't read Portuguese so we have to rely on you."

"Of course!" she said. "You must start out with a drink first—a caipirinha. Very Brazilian."

"What's in it?" Janice asked. "I had one at the hotel yesterday, and it was fantastic. Cool and delicious. But I never found out what they put in it."

"Very simple," Natalia said. "Just lime and sugar and cachaca."

"What's cachaca?" Mary Louise asked.

"It's a liquor distilled from sugar cane," Natalia said. "Only found here in Brazil. They use rum in other places, but it's not the same." She waved to the waiter standing nearby.

"Felipe," she said. "Six caipirinhas, *por favor.*"

"Just five, Natalia," I said. "I'll have water, please."

"You come to Rio and drink water!" Natalia said. "No, is not possible. You must have a caipirinha!"

It used to bother me when people insisted on giving me a drink when I first gave it up, but now I'm used to it—pretty much.

"No, really, Natalia," I said softly. "I've given it up. I really just want water." Not exactly the truth. I definitely wanted a caipirinha, but I'm learning. One day at a time.

Her expression changed. She got it. And being Natalia, she found something good about not drinking.

"Fewer calories!" she said. "No wonder you're in such good shape, Pat. I should give it up too."

"Tell us about the menu, Natalia," Gini said. "What should we order?"

"Felipe," Natalia said to the waiter as he put the drinks in front of us. "Bring us some pão de queijo and some calabresa sausages to start—oh, and some pastelzinhos too. Please."

She practically rose out of her chair with delight as she ordered these appetizers. "Oh, oh, you will love these," she said. "The pão de queijo are little cheese puffs, little chewy things that you eat along with the spicy, garlicky calabresa sausages, and the pastelzinhos are crispy turnovers filled with tomatoes and olives."

"Sounds like a whole meal, Natalia," Mary Louise says. "Aren't they kind of heavy?"

"No, not at all," Natalia said. "They're little yummies. You'll see. And then—"

"Why don't we start with the appetizers," Tina said, "and then see if we have room for the main course."

Natalia sighed. "Americans," she said. "Always watching your figures."

"No, no, it's not that," Tina said. "We have to dance tonight, and we don't want to eat too much. You understand."

"I do understand," she said. "I always eat a lot anyway."

"Well, how do you eat so much and stay so thin?" Gini asked.

"I just eat one meal a day," she said. "That's

all I need. And I dance a lot. That gets rid of tons of calories."

The waiter brought the drinks. I was surprised to find that I didn't yearn for a caipirinha. I wasn't crazy about my glass of water either, but I could live with it. It's hard to stop wanting liquor when it's been a big part of your life. For so long, a drink at the end of the day was my way of relaxing, of letting go of other people's problems after a day of counseling clients. A little bourbon and water on the rocks. Or a glass of white wine. Sometimes a sweet vermouth with lemon. A beer on a hot day. I didn't really think there was anything wrong with this habit until one day I couldn't stop. I just kept drinking instead of eating supper and stumbled into bed and fell into a deep sleep. When I woke up, I couldn't remember the last part of the day before.

Then I began having a drink earlier and earlier. One morning I woke up and had a drink before my coffee. My friends noticed. They made a few tactful comments, but they left me alone until I realized I had a problem. I started going to Alcoholics Anonymous where a sponsor helped me through the first weeks. I hadn't realized how much I relied on alcohol to get through difficult days. It took a while—a whole year in fact until I could go to bed sober every night. What a difference it made in my life. I had more energy. My brain worked better. I was calmer.

Don't get me wrong. I still want a drink when things are really difficult, but most of the time, I don't go back. It also helps being with Denise. She stopped drinking when she came to live with me to make it easier for me, and she always had something interesting planned for us to do at the end of the day. She still has an occasional drink when we go out to dinner or to a party at a friend's house, but she claims she doesn't miss a drink or two every day. I love her very much.

But those caipirinhas did look good.

Gini, who can read my mind, saw me take a sip of the water. "Drinking straight vodka again, Pat?" she said and winked at me.

"Yes," I said, smiling at my funny friend. "Can't believe you're drinking that insipid little distilled sugar thing."

"We don't all have your hollow leg, Pat," Janice said.

Did I tell you I treasure these women? They're always supportive when it counts. I value their friendship more than gold.

Natalia, who didn't really get the whole thing, looked around nervously. I could imagine her thinking, *"Oh, never mind, they're Americans. Who knows what they're talking about?"*

The waiter brought the appetizers, and they were incredibly good.

"You have to eat them in a certain way," Natalia said. "You must alternate bites of the pão de queijo, the cheese puffs, with the calabresa sausages, which are really spicy and garlicky. It's the contrast of the two textures that brings out the best in each one. And in between those two, you nibble on the pastelzinhos, which are crispy, some filled with unmelted cheese, some with beef, tomatoes, and olives."

We followed her instructions. She was right. The different flavors and textures were sublime.

When the appetizers were almost gone, Natalia said, "You can't stop now! I won't allow it. You must have their picadinho before you go."

Tina looked around the table at her fellow Hoofers and could tell we wanted to try whatever this was. I mean, when would we be back in Rio again?

"OK. Six pica—whatever you called it—please, waiter."

While we finished the last few bites of our crunchy turnovers, Gini tried again.

"Tell us more about Maria, Natalia," she said. "We only spent a short time with her and didn't really get to know her. What was she like?"

Natalia took a sip of her caipirinha and fiddled around with her silverware before she answered. Her face was serious. "Maria was my friend," she said. "She had a horrible marriage with that Lucas. She used to cry all the time. He cheated on her from their honeymoon on, and she was miserable. Finally she had enough and divorced him. The court awarded her alimony—quite a bit—and Lucas would either pay a small part of it or nothing. Maria had to take him to court all the time to get her money. I wouldn't be surprised if . . ."

"If what?" Gini said. We were all listening intently.

"Oh, I shouldn't . . . Don't pay any attention to me. I didn't like Lucas because of the way he treated Maria. But I don't really know if . . ."

It wasn't hard to guess what she was going to say. Gini leaned forward to ask another question, but before she could speak, the waiter brought the picadinho.

One bite and I had to finish this delicious beef dish, flavored with garlic and onion and green pepper and tomatoes and I don't know what all. It wasn't exactly a light dish, but who cared. We all gobbled it up and skipped any more discussion of Maria and Lucas. Mary Louise, of course, had to know how to make it.

"Natalia," she said, "this picadinho is superb. Could you get the recipe from the chef here please?"

Natalia almost turned inside out with delight at the change in subject. This she could understand. "Better than that, my little Hoofer. When we get back to the hotel, I'll ask our chef to show you how they make it and give you the recipe. His name is Luiz, and he's a darling. He'd do anything for me."

"I'd love that, Natalia," Mary Louise said. "How do you say 'thank you' again?

" *'Obrigada'* if you're a woman and *'obrigado'* if you're a man."

"Then *mucho obrigada,*" Mary Louise said.

The waiter came back to our table as we finished our meal and asked if we wanted dessert.

Tina waved her hand. "I think we'd better

stop here," she said. "We'll waddle onto the stage tonight and collapse if we eat any more."

I could have used a little Brazilian dessert, but of course Tina was right. We followed her out to the van after paying the bill.

Back at the hotel, Natalia flibbertigibbeted into the kitchen talking all the time to Mary Louise, whom she dragged along with her. A few minutes later, she came out again and said Luiz would be happy to show us how to make the picadinho.

"We can rehearse later, Tina?" Natalia said, making her question into a statement.

Tina smiled. She's the most flexible woman on earth. "Come on, Hoofers, let's go see Luiz."

Luiz was a tall, jolly man in his thirties, slim and spotless in a white apron and chef's hat. He bowed when we came into his large, very clean kitchen and said in slightly accented English, "Welcome, my dancers. Natalia says you would like to learn to make my picadinho. I am making it for dinner tonight so you will get to eat it again later. It has to cook long time, but I show you the first part now. Come closer."

Even Gini, who hates cooking, couldn't resist this handsome man who obviously loved what he did.

"First," Luiz said, "you must brown a chopped-up onion and some garlic in olive oil in this large, deep saucepan. I have already chopped."

While they were browning, he pulled out a large bowl. "In this bowl, I have put some beef—really good beef like sirloin or filet—stirred-up eggs, chopped celery, green pepper, parsley, peas and canned tomatoes."

"You use canned tomatoes?" Mary Louise asked, surprised. "I thought all chefs used fresh tomatoes. I always feel guilty when I used canned ones at home."

"It does not matter that they are canned," Luiz said. "They are the very best plum tomatoes. You will like. But if you insist on fresh tomatoes, don't use the large, tasteless ones. Get the fresh small tomatoes, preferably plum tomatoes."

He mixed together all the ingredients in the bowl until they were thoroughly combined. When the onions and garlic were a delicious-looking brown color, he added the mixture in the bowl to the saucepan and cooked them until they, too, were brown, stirring all the time.

"Now," he said, "we add some salt and pepper and red wine—be sure it's a dry red wine. I use Portuguese wines, but you can use a cabernet or a pinot noir, anything dry. Now I cover our pan and cook for about fifteen minutes."

While the wine was flavoring the ingredients, he asked us where we were from. We told him we lived in New Jersey.

"You go to New York?" he asked.

"We love New York," Janice said.

"What does such a beautiful woman do in New York?" Luiz asked.

"Everything that's legal," Janice said, making him laugh. "I love the theater and good restaurants. I go to museums and baseball games, walk in Central Park, ice skate in Rockefeller Center, ride on the carousel in Bryant Park and the one in Brooklyn. You should come there. I'll take you on a private tour."

"Lovely lady, I would follow you anywhere," Luiz said, leaning across the counter to kiss Janice's hand. See why we keep her around?

When the wine had done its job, Luiz added some more wine and red pepper flakes, and put the cover partly back on.

"Now this must cook for an hour to let the wine disappear into the picadinho. Then I add some green olives, some capers, maybe pimento, raisins—whatever I feel like—and cook them just long enough to heat them. Tonight, before you dance, I bring it to you to eat."

"Small portions please, Luiz," Tina said. "We're already full from a sensational lunch, and we're dancing a samba. We need to be able to move."

"Do not worry, senhora," he said. "I will give you just a taste, so you can enchant our guests with your dance."

"*Obrigada,*" Tina said. That was becoming our favorite word in this land of gracious living and generous offers.

"It smells divine, Luiz," Mary Louise said. "Any chance you could give me the recipe?"

"Of course, my little American housewife," Luiz said. "I will have it sent to your room."

Mary Louise gave him a hug—she always hugs people—and we left the kitchen to change into rehearsal clothes.

Picadinho
Serves four.

⅓ cup olive oil
1 onion, chopped
3 cloves garlic, chopped
2 lbs. lean ground beef—sirloin or fillet
6 eggs, beaten
2 ribs celery, chopped
1 green pepper, chopped
1 cup chopped parsley
2 35 oz cans of plum tomatoes
½ cup green olives
1 tsp. capers
1 tbsp. chopped pimento
1 cup peas
½ cup raisins
Salt and ground pepper
1½ cups dry red wine
¼ tsp. hot red pepper flakes—not too much

1. Brown the onion and garlic in the olive oil in a large, deep saucepan.
2. In a medium-sized bowl, mix the beef, eggs, and the next nine ingredients together.
3. Add the meat mixture to the saucepan with the onion and garlic and cook over medium flame until the meat is a light brown, stirring all the time.
4. Cook for twenty minutes.
5. Add salt and pepper and a cup of the wine.

Cover, reduce heat and cook for another fifteen minutes.

6. Sprinkle with the red pepper flakes (remember, not too much—about ¼ tsp), and add the other half cup of wine.

7. Cover partially and cook for an hour and fifteen minutes. Stir every once in a while.

8. Enjoy!

Pat's Tip for Traveling with Friends: Decide, before you go, how much money you want to spend on this trip and make sure your friend agrees.

Chapter Five

Slow Down!!!

When Gini and I got to our room, I said, "You were right about your feelings about Lucas. You said you didn't like him. Natalia practically accused him of killing Maria to keep from paying her alimony."

"I don't know, Pat. Seems a little drastic, doesn't it? But I definitely didn't like him—or that woman he was with on the beach. Who was that again?"

"I think her name is Yasmin. She said she was the hotel accountant. We can ask Natalia about her."

I laughed. Thinking of Natalia always makes

me laugh. "I can't make up my mind about Natalia," I said. "Is she really that ditzy, or is she a lot smarter than we think she is?"

"Hard to tell," Gini said. "I know what you mean though. One minute she seems like an absolute idiot. The next she sounds really intelligent. I have a feeling that the clowning around is an act so that other people won't realize how really smart she is. I'm sure she knows a lot more about what's going on around here than she lets on."

"Like when she was talking about Lucas. She sure doesn't care for him."

"She doesn't seem to. Come on. Let's go rehearse. Maybe we can find out more."

We changed into shorts and sleeveless tops and went back to the piano bar to join the rest of our group.

Natalia, hair perfectly arranged, makeup restored to its full power, dressed in a white halter top and tight white pants, greeted us.

"Ah, Gini and Pat. Now we are all here. I want you to meet Felipe, who will play the piano for us, Joao, who is our trumpeter, Tiago on cello, and Mateus on drums."

The musicians hung back a little, not sure of how to greet us. But our Tina shook hands and chatted a little with each one of them, and they relaxed a little. They didn't really speak much English, but we managed to let them know that we appreciated them and were glad they would be playing for us. They were all in their twenties and thirties, with various shades of brown skin, from Felipe who was the darkest to Tiago who was the lightest.

"We will practice the samba first, yes?" Natalia said.

As usual, with Natalia, it was a statement not a question. She knew what she wanted and the rest of us followed along.

For once we had a floor big enough to move on without bumping into each other. The samba started and we moved with it. It was basically a step to the right and a ball change, with the left foot in back and then forward. It was easy to get into the rhythm and we abandoned ourselves to the music, swinging our hips Latino-style. *Mucho* hips. Natalia sang some song in Portuguese that kept using the word *Copacabana,* We didn't really care what the words were. It was the acceleration of the samba. The excitement of it. The feeling that the music ruled us, not the other way around. It was exhilarating. We finished—sweating, laughing, and delighted.

Loud applause when we stopped. Miguel was standing in front of us clapping and cheering for us.

"*Legal,*" he said, pronouncing it lay-gah-oo, which Natalia said meant *cool.* "You will be a sensation tonight."

"Thanks, Miguel," Gini said. "I hope the temperature will be a little cooler too."

"Me too," I said. "I need a swim. Anybody else?"

"I come with you," Natalia said. "Meet me by the water."

"I want a cold drink," Gini said. "All that sambaing made me thirsty. I think I'll skip the swim for now. See you later, Pat."

The others joined Gini at the bar. I headed for the elevator but noticed an elegant little gift shop off the lobby. Besides the tasteful jewelry on the counter, there were sandals, some cosmetics, bathing suits and cover-ups, and other small items guests might find appealing. I decided to try to buy another bathing suit. One more like the others I saw on the beach.

"*Hola, senhora,*" the pretty young girl behind the counter said. She had a beautiful smile that lit up her face.

"*Hola,*" I said. "I'd like to find a bathing suit. So I'll look more Brazilian. You know?"

"I know exactly what you mean, senhora," she said. "Something like this perhaps?" She picked up a blue and green infinitesimal top with an almost nonexistent thong, which was probably blue and green too. I wanted it. I would never be able to wear it back home. If I ever ventured out on the beach in Harwich Port on Cape Cod, people would probably have me arrested. And anyway, I'd freeze to death in the cold Nantucket Sound. What the heck.

"How much?" I asked.

"Only one hundred and ten dollars, senhora. A real bargain."

One hundred and ten dollars! For about six

inches of material. If I had any sense, I'd just go upstairs and put on one of the bathing suits I brought with me. Luckily, I had no sense.

"I'll take it," I said. Well, I was in Rio. You were supposed to ignore all the rules in this city. You do realize how hard this was for me. Old stick-in-the-mud, follow-the-rules Pat. Not today.

I gave the girl my credit card, and she wrapped this overpriced, extravagant excuse for a bathing suit in a miniature Copacabana shopping bag and handed it to me. "Enjoy, senhora," she said. She probably could have fed her whole family for a month on what that suit cost.

My guilty conscience that was always there ready to yell at me for anything my mother wouldn't have approved of, tried to shame me all the way up in the elevator, but it didn't seem to have the power to destroy me that it usually had. Must be Rio.

My cell phone was tootling as I entered the suite.

"Pat, it's me," Denise said when I answered. It was so good to hear her voice. I felt as if she were in the next room instead of back home in New Jersey. "What's happening? How are you? How's Rio? I miss you."

"Hello, love," I said. "It's good to hear your voice. I just spent way too much on a teensy bathing suit, but I don't care. Well, I almost don't care. Tell me it was OK."

"Of course, it's OK, you ninny. I just wish I could be there to see you in it."

"So do I, Denise. How are you?"

"I'm fine," she said. "But your little cat, Eliza, keeps running to the door every time it opens to see if you've come home. She looks at me accusingly whenever it's someone else. She thinks I've done away with you. She curls up next to your pillow every night. So do I, actually."

"I love that little cat," I said. "I miss her too. Give her a big hug from me."

"I will, sweetie, but what's this I hear about a murder in your hotel? Can't you go anywhere without causing some poor person's death?"

"How did you know about that?" I asked. "I wasn't going to tell you. I didn't want you to worry."

"It was on CNN today. 'Murder at the Copacabana.' Sounds like a movie from the forties. Who was it, who did it, and are you safe there?"

"Don't worry, hon," I said. "I'm perfectly safe. Somebody killed our guide—poisoned her, I think—but we don't know who did it yet. They don't tell us very much. The police chief is very nice, but he doesn't discuss the details of the murder with us. I don't blame him. Listen, Denise, you have to come to this hotel. I mean sometime when nobody gets murdered. You and David. It's incredibly beautiful. The beach is gorgeous—I'm on my way there now. You'd love it. And so would David. How is he?"

"He's doing well, Pat, I'm happy to say. Since you came to live with us, you've been a tremendous help giving him more confidence. He's not so shy in school anymore. He's taking part in more activities and making more friends. You did that. I'll always love you for what you've done for him."

"He's a wonderful boy, Denise. I think of him as my son, too, you know."

"I know," she said. "Wish we were there with you now. Come home soon, my love."

"I'll be there before you know it," I said. "I'll talk to you later."

"Try not to cause any more murders," she said and hung up.

I put on my new bathing suit. I checked my stomach in the full-length mirror. We've been eating so much fattening food here that I expected to see a little bulge over the thong. But I was OK. Must be all that dancing and sweating.

I grabbed a bottle of water from the minibar in our suite. When I got to the beach, I saw Natalia's red-blond hair down by the water. She was lying on a towel, like most of the women around her. I almost dropped my bottle of water when I saw her body. She was rubbing lotion on her legs, and I had to keep saying Denise's name over and over to keep my cool.

She looked up as I put my towel on the sand next to her.

"May I join you?" I asked.

"Please do," she said. "You are very beautiful." She sat up and held her lotion out to me. "Don't burn that gorgeous body."

Was she coming on to me or was I just imagining it?

She reached around behind me and unfastened my top. "Don't hide them," she said, very close to me.

Nope. I wasn't imagining it.

"Uh, Natalia, I live with someone," I said, refastening my bra. "And you know perfectly well topless bathing isn't allowed on the beaches in Rio."

"So?" she said, her eyes watching me. "Nobody will arrest you."

I stood up. "I will," I said. "Think I'll go in the water." I couldn't handle this. This little bundle of joy was going way beyond the accepted limits.

She laughed. "I'll be here when you come out," she said.

I ran into the water and swam without stopping for a few minutes. The cool water felt heavenly. I tried not to think about Natalia. I might as well have tried not to think about my sunburned nose. How could I discourage her without insulting her? I must have given her some signal without meaning to that I was open to her advances.

This wasn't like Captain Chantal, the chief of police in Paris, to whom I was attracted when we were there. She and I were both involved with other people, so we were careful to keep our relationship friendly. She was even coming to New York to stay with Denise and me in a couple of months. But Natalia. She was an entirely different smorgasbord. I had to turn her off somehow.

I swam back to the shore, slowly, smoothly, figuring out what I would say.

I lay down on my towel and said, "Natalia . . .
I . . ."

She sat up and patted my hand. "Don't worry,
sweetheart. I'm not trying to seduce you. I know
you're involved with someone else. But you
can't blame me for trying. You're so attractive.
And that's some suit!"

I was relieved. I sat up too. "Thanks for understanding, Natalia. Denise and I are very close.
But there's no reason you and I can't be friends."

She smiled. "Count on it, honey," she said.

We both lay back down and soaked up the
Rio sun. It was life restoring. I thought Natalia
had fallen asleep, but after about ten minutes,
she said, "Did you know Maria was having an affair with Miguel?"

I pushed my sunglasses up on my forehead
and looked at her. "The hotel manager? No.
Tell me."

Natalia moved closer and said in a low voice,
"They didn't even try to hide it. Sumiko—you
know, Miguel's wife—was furious. But Sumiko
was having an affair with the hotel doctor—Dr.
Souza—so she didn't really care. She was just
mad that Maria and Miguel were so open about
their fooling around. She didn't like being hu-
miliated."

"How did Maria die?" I asked. "No one has
told us that."

"They're not sure," she said. "They think she
was given some kind of drug, but there was no
trace of it in her body. They just found her lying
there on her bed. At first they thought she must

have had a heart attack, but the medical examiner said no. They really don't know what killed her."

"That's weird," I said.

"Everything in Rio is weird," Natalia said, laughing her musical laugh.

If I didn't love Denise . . .

"I thought you were from Rio," I said.

"No, from São Paulo. It's much better than Rio."

"What do you mean?"

"São Paulo is a serious place. Cosmopolitan. Smart people live and work there. Rio is just for fun, for vacations, for fooling around. Sort of like the difference between New York and Hollywood. You get things done in New York. Hollywood is like a temporary break from the real world. Know what I mean?"

"Sure. But as a singer, I would think you'd prefer Rio."

"Oh, I live here because that's where I get the most work. But as a place to spend my life, I prefer São Paulo. As soon as I get enough money saved, I'm going back there."

"Do you have family there?"

"My dad and my sisters." Her face closed down. It was clear she didn't want to talk about her family.

"We'd better get back," I said. "We have to eat, dress, and dance, and I'm all icky."

"Want me to help you with your bath?" Natalia said, dodging my swipe at her with my towel. "Kidding, just kidding.""

We went back to the hotel and Gini had already changed into a pale green silk dress that was perfect with her dark red hair.

"Wow!" she said when she saw my bathing suit. "Pat? Is that you? You look fantastic. Is that suit new?"

"Yeah, I got it in the shop downstairs. Oh, Gini, it cost a hundred and ten dollars! My mother would kill me."

"Your mother is dead," Gini said. "You're allowed to spend a hundred and ten dollars on a bathing suit if you can afford it."

"Actually, I can't really afford it. But there's something about Rio that . . . ."

"I know what you mean," Gini said. "Everything seems to be accepted here."

"Good thing we're only going to be here a few more days," I said, "or I'd be broke. Go ahead down to the restaurant if you want, Gini. I'll shower and dress and come down later."

"I'm not sure I can eat any more after that lunch today," Gini said. "But Miguel said we have to try the moqueca—a seafood stew—even if we only take a couple of bites. We don't have to dance until nine so I'm going to try it."

"I thought Luiz was going to give us the picadinho he made for us today in the kitchen."

"I guess he changed his mind and wanted us to try the moqueca," Gini said. "I'll eat anything he cooks. He's a genius."

"Yeah, who cares?" I said, going into the luxurious bathroom. "We may never have the chance to eat moqueca again."

"Rio is having a really good effect on you, Pat," she said and left.

I showered and slipped into my favorite blue lace dress, white stilettos, and dangly pearl earrings and went downstairs to the Pergula Restaurant, an elegant dining room overlooking the swimming pool.

Everyone was seated, including my new friend, Natalia, who was next to Yasmin, the woman Gini and I met at the beach the day before. Her eyes, without the sunglasses hiding them, were so dark they were almost black.

She was much friendlier today than she had been at the beach. "*Boa noite,* Pat," she said, wishing me a good evening and reaching over to shake hands with me. "Did you have a good swim?"

"*Boa noite,*" I said. "Yes, fine, thank you. This beach is probably the most beautiful I've ever been to. And the water is just the right temperature—not too cold."

"I know," she said. "I sneak off for a quick swim every chance I get."

"What do you do here?" Janice asked.

"I'm in charge of finances," she said. "Sort of a glorified accountant. I don't really have a title."

"We couldn't get along without her," Miguel said, stopping by our table to greet us and put his hand on her shoulder. "We are looking forward to your performance tonight, senhoras."

"We're looking forward to your moqueca, Senhor Ortega," Tina said. "But could you please ask the chef to give us small portions. We don't want to waddle instead of dance."

"Small portions it will be," Ortega said. "And just a small caipirinha to start. It will make you dance even better."

"Six caipirinhas and one water, please," our thoughtful Tina said, glancing at me.

The manager left us, and Natalia, sexy in a red, backless dress, asked, "Did you like the trip to Corcovado, my little Hoofers?"

We all talked at once, telling her how meaningful it had been for us.

"I'll never forget it, Natalia," I said. "It was truly memorable."

"Where are you taking us tomorrow?" Mary Louise asked.

"To another mountain—Sugar Loaf. There are beautiful gardens and a view of the city you won't want to miss."

"Sounds like a great place for photos," Gini said, raising her caipirinha the waiter had just put in front of us in a toast. *"Vive Rio!"*

We all toasted Rio, and I sipped my water while the rest drank their cocktails. Sometimes I get really sick of water, and this was one of those times. I motioned to the waiter. "Do you have anything more exciting than water that doesn't have liquor in it?" I asked him in a low voice.

"Why don't you try some coconut water and lime juice?" he asked. "Many of our Muslim friends who do not drink enjoy that."

I almost kissed him. "Yes, please," I said.

He returned in a few minutes with my coconut water, which was deliciously refreshing.

"I want to see some of the nightlife in Rio," Janice said. "You know, Natalia—some nightclubs and stuff. Will you give us a tour of those?"

"Anytime you want," she said. "That's my specialty." She grinned.

The waiter brought our moqueca, a kind of seafood stew. I took a bite, not expecting it to be that great. Actually, it was so delicious, I beat Mary Louise to a request for the recipe from Natalia.

"Of course, my love," she said. "I'll bring it to your room myself." She winked at me, and I smiled back at this wicked little singer who loved to make trouble.

"OK, Hoofers," Tina said when we had eaten every bite of this marvel, "we've got to get back to our rooms and change for our dance tonight. Hope you're not too full."

Gini made a mock groaning noise and said, "Oh, Tina, I'm so full I can't possibly dance. You'll have to go on without me."

Tina is used to Gini. "That's all right, Gini," she said. "We'll split up your part of our salary for ourselves. You can heave your fat body onto your bed and sleep while we're dancing."

We all laughed. We knew the word *fat* would send Gini into a sputtering rage. "Who are you calling fat?" she squawked. "I'm skinnier than all of you!"

We gathered her up and scooped her onto the elevator where she calmed down. I followed her in, and we went upstairs to change into red samba gowns that would show off our hips to best advantage when we danced this fast, sexy dance.

Moqueca

For the soup:

2 lbs. swordfish, cut into large pieces
3 cloves minced garlic
4 tbsps. lime juice
Salt and freshly ground pepper
2 tbsps. olive oil
1 cup medium-sized onion, sliced
½ yellow pepper, sliced
½ red pepper, sliced
1 tbsp. paprika
Pinch red pepper flakes
Salt and pepper, to taste
2 cups quartered plum tomatoes
¼ cup chopped green onion greens
1 large bunch of chopped cilantro
1 14-oz. can coconut milk

For the rice:

1 tbsp. olive oil
½ onion chopped
1 clove minced garlic

1 cup white rice
1½ cups boiling water
1 tsp. salt

1. Salt and pepper the swordfish pieces and chill them in a bowl with the garlic and lime juice while you make the rice and the soup. Set aside.

2. Heat the olive oil in a saucepan on medium heat. Add the onion and cook until it's transparent. Add the garlic and cook for another minute.

3. Add the rice and mix with the onion and garlic.

4. Pour in the boiling water and one teaspoon salt. Simmer rice for fifteen minutes.When it's done, put it aside to serve with the soup.

5. For the soup, heat two tablespoons olive oil in a Dutch oven.

6. Add the onion and cook until soft.

7. Add the sliced yellow and red peppers, paprika and red pepper flakes, salt and pepper. Cook until peppers are soft.

8. Add chopped plum tomatoes and onion greens and cook for five minutes, uncovered. Add handful of cilantro.

9. With a slotted spoon, take out half the vegetables and put on a plate.

10. Spread the other half of the vegetables over the bottom of the pan.

11. Salt and pepper the swordfish pieces and place them on top of the vegetables in the pan.

12. Put the reserved vegetables on top of the swordfish.

13. Pour the coconut milk over everything.

14. When the coconut milk is simmering, turn down the heat, cover, and let it cook slowly for fifteen minutes.

15. Sprinkle with the cilantro and serve with the rice.

16. Enjoy!!!

Pat's Tip for Traveling with Friends: If your friend hates shopping in flea markets, get a new friend.

Chapter Six

Sing, Samba, Swim

The room was full of guests from the hotel. When we appeared in our red dresses, our hips moving to the samba the band was playing, they applauded. As we danced faster and faster, we were astonished to see some of the audience get up and start to samba next to their tables. This had never happened to us before. I remembered that Maria had said to us at one point, "Brazilians live to dance." Now I believed it.

It was fantastic seeing them move like that, as if they couldn't help dancing to the music. It revved up our own excitement in this incredible samba. We clapped as we danced, and I felt we were applauding our audience. Natalia matched the mood with her singing of "Copacabana," and we ended up with a blast of joy and *"Olés!"* from the guests.

We bowed and were surrounded by people congratulating us.

"Come, I must dance with you," a gray-haired, handsome man said, putting his arm around my waist and leading me back onto the floor.

I didn't have time to say "yes, "no," or "wait a second." I was being swirled into something that was very Latin, but I had no idea what I was doing. I just followed this man who held me very close and guided me firmly, expertly, to the music played by the band. He didn't smile, just danced as if he was sure I could follow him. I was amazed to find that I could, no matter what he did. No man had ever danced with me like that before.

When the music stopped, he twirled me around, dipped me over backward, and kissed me lightly on the forehead. When I straightened up, he let me go, bowed, and said, "Gabriel Souza at your service, senhora."

"Dr. Souza?" I said. "The doctor for the hotel?"

"I am," he said. "And you are?"

"I'm Pat Keeler," I said. "A Happy Hoofer, not really at your service."

He laughed. "I'm disappointed to hear that, senhora. We dance so perfectly together."

"I'll dance with you anytime," I said, taking his hand and leading him over to the rest of our group.

"Hey, Hoofers, I want you to meet Dr. Souza. He dances like Fred Astaire."

My friends all said hello, and of course, my gorgeous doctor forgot all the rest of us when he saw Janice. He took her hand and led her onto the floor when the band started to play again. He didn't ask, just assumed she would be glad to dance with him, which of course, she was. It was some kind of fast Latin music again, and Janice followed him easily. Oh, well, it was fun while it lasted.

It didn't last long for Janice either. Just as the doctor and Janice were really getting into it, Sumiko strode onto the floor, tapped the doctor on the shoulder, lightly pushed Janice out of the way, and took her place.

Janice came back to join us. "Whooooa," she said. "That Sumiko doesn't fool around. She took over that doctor as if she owned him."

"Natalia said she does own him," I said in a low voice. "She's fooling around with him. There seems to be a lot of that going on in this hotel."

"You better believe it," Natalia said, slipping in beside me.

"I'm totally confused," Mary Louise said. "Who's having an affair with whom?"

"It is confusing," Natalia said. "Let me straighten all this out for you. Why don't you change into your bathing suits and join me in the pool to get cooled off. Then I'll tell you everything."

We were all sweating like crazy, so her suggestion to go for a swim was a great idea. We went to our rooms and put on swimsuits. When we got back to the pool, Natalia was already paddling around in the clear, cool water in an almost nonexistent suit. The hotel guests were still dancing to the never-ending band music. They didn't seem surprised when the five of us in almost no clothes scooted by them and dove into the pool. They only glanced at us briefly. It was as if they were used to things like this happening all the time. I was beginning to believe Natalia's description of Rio—anything can happen there. People just expect it.

We treaded water in the deep end away from any eavesdroppers and gathered around Natalia.

"OK, Natalia, give," Gini said.

"First of all," Natalia said, "Maria was sleeping with Miguel, the hotel manager. Miguel's wife, Sumiko, is fooling around with Dr. Souza. Yasmin, the accountant, is having an affair with Lucas, Maria's ex-husband. Maria hated Lucas so she didn't really care who he slept with. I know all this because I have had occasional flings with Maria, Souza, Yasmin, and Miguel, who sleeps with everybody."

We all burst out laughing. This outrageous little person was the best part of our whole Rio adventure.

"So who killed Maria?" Gini asked.

Natalia said, "Come closer."

We splashed up near her. She looked around to make sure no one could hear her and said, "I think it was Sumiko." She checked to make sure Sumiko was still sambaing with the doctor.

"See, Souza is an anesthesiologist. Somebody obviously gave Maria some kind of anesthetic that disappears from the body so it can't be traced. I Googled anesthetics and found out there's this stuff called succinylcholine chloride that kills and then very conveniently melts away somewhere, and the medical examiner can't find it. It's an anesthetic. Souza is an anesthesiologist. Get it? I think Sumiko got some from the doctor and used it on Maria."

"You think the doctor is involved in her death too?" I asked.

"I'm not sure," Natalia said, "whether he gave Sumiko the anesthetic or she stole it from him."

"But why would Sumiko want to kill Maria?" Gini asked.

"Because she was afraid her husband was getting serious about Maria, and would divorce her. Sumiko loves to fool around but she doesn't want to end her marriage. She likes the life and the money she has here, and she isn't about to give it up to marry some hotel doctor. So she decided to get rid of Maria."

"Couldn't she just get her fired?" Gini asked. "Seems a bit over the top to kill her."

"Even if she were fired, her husband could keep seeing her," Natalia said. "Sumiko wanted her out of the way permanently."

"I don't know," Gini said. "It just doesn't seem likely. You don't kill somebody to keep her from having an affair with your husband."

"Well, who do you think did it?" Natalia asked her.

"I'm not sure," Gini said. "What about Lucas, Maria's ex? At lunch I got the impression you thought Lucas killed Maria so he wouldn't have to pay her any more alimony. That seems more logical to me. "

"I did think it was Lucas at first," she said, "but I just don't think he has the guts to do it. Oops. Dummy up, guys. Miguel is coming this way."

I'm telling you—if I didn't love Denise so much, I would definitely have fun with this cute little singer.

Miguel leaned down to talk to us in the pool.

"Your dancing was superb," he said. "Our guests loved you."

"It was so great seeing them dance too," Tina said. "That's never happened to us before. Do they always do that?"

"Not like tonight," Miguel said. "They really liked you."

"Come join us, Miguelito," Natalia said, flicking some water at him.

"Natalia, you know I can't get in the pool now. I'm working."

"Too bad," she said. "You're missing all the fun."

"Life is not always fun, Natalia," he said sternly.

"Who says?" she said and grabbed both his ankles. When he fell, she pulled him into the pool and pushed his head under the water.

He came up sputtering, furious at her. Even I thought she had gone too far this time.

"You're fired!" he said, climbing out of the pool, dripping water on the dance floor as he went to his room to change into dry clothes.

"He doesn't mean it," Natalia said. "He fires me all the time, but then forgets about it when I sing. He loves my voice—among other things."

I didn't want to leave the pool because there was no telling what would happen with this sassy little broad around, but it looked like the party was over. I swam a few laps before toweling off and going back to my room.

Pat's Tip for Traveling with Friends: If you're not a shopper and your friend is, pretend you are and you might find something you want.

Chapter Seven

And a Very Bom Dia to You

I woke up early the next morning and wanted to go for a walk but remembered all the warnings about roaming around Rio by myself. Not a good idea, according to all accounts. Gini was still fast asleep, so I dressed quickly and quietly and sneaked down to the breakfast room for some coffee.

I was enjoying a delicious, strong, hot cup of coffee and a roll when Yasmin approached my table. "May I join you?" she said.

"Please do," I said, surprised to see her.

She looked fresh and cool in a black and white striped top and pants. Her hair was pulled back, tied with a pale green scarf.

"You're up early," she said.

"I just couldn't sleep anymore," I said. "I'd love to walk around outside for a while, but they said not to do that—too dangerous. Is that true?"

"You don't have to worry at this hour of the day," she said. "I don't have to start work for a while. Would you like me to come with you and point out some things about Rio?"

"I'd love it," I said. "That's so nice of you. Are you sure you have time?"

"Oh, yes," she said. "I always have time. Things are very relaxed around here."

We left the hotel and walked along the streets crowded with cafés and small clothing shops just starting to open.

"Are you from Rio, Yasmin?" I asked.

"No. São Paulo. Much more serious than Rio. But I love the music and the—I don't know—the lightheartedness of this city."

"But your work is so serious," I said.

"You mean because I'm an accountant?" she asked and laughed. "It's not all that serious."

"I guess I always associate anything to do with money and finance with grimness," I said. "I'm not much good at it myself. I wish I were. I'm always worried about money."

"You should move to Rio, Pat," she said. "We don't take anything very seriously. Brazilians just want everything to turn out all right, and if necessary, we help things along so they *will* turn out all right. *Comprende?*"

"Good philosophy, Yasmin," I said. "My clients should follow that philosophy."

"Your clients?" she asked.

"Yes, I'm a family therapist, and my clients always think the worst is going to happen. And it usually does. It's as if they wish it on themselves. A large part of my job is helping them think more positively—about themselves and about their situation. "

"You have to make life happen the way *you* want it to happen," she said. She was quiet for a minute. Then she added, "No matter what."

I looked at her. She was lost in another world. As if I weren't there. What was going on in that mathematical brain? I wondered. Everybody in this hotel seemed to have some kind of secret.

I wasn't paying much attention to the little shops we passed until I saw a silk blouse that was perfect for Denise hanging outside one of the stores. It was a pale lavender and would be beautiful with her dark hair and blue eyes. I stopped to look at it more closely. Yasmin kept walking, looking down at the ground, absorbed in thought, until she realized I was no longer with her. She came back to the shop.

"Sorry, Pat," she said. "I got caught up in my thoughts."

"I noticed," I said. "What were you thinking about so deeply?"

"Nothing much really. Just about the work I have waiting for me back at the office. I suppose I should be getting back."

"Go ahead if you want. I'm going to buy this blouse for my girlfriend."

"Is this a serious relationship or just a friend/ friend thing?" she asked.

"Very serious," I said. "We live together with her son, David."

"You're lucky to have someone to love," she said. "I'm still looking. He'll come along one of these days."

"I thought you and Lucas were serious about each other," I said. "When you were with him at the beach you two seemed to be more than just friends. Did I just imagine that?"

"Yes, you did," she said. "We go out together sometimes, but we're not really a couple. He's not easy to be with. Very negative. I want somebody much better than Lucas."

"I'm sure you'll meet him soon," I said. "You're such an attractive woman."

"For an accountant?" Yasmin said and laughed.

"Right," I said.

She helped me haggle with the owner of the shop for a proper price for the blouse.

"Don't ever pay the first price they quote you in these little shops," she said. "They expect you to argue them down. It's different when you are in one of the department stores, though. Their price is set and you're not supposed to try to get a lower one."

I bought the blouse for Denise, paying much less than I would have paid at home and less than I would have paid if Yasmin hadn't been with me. We headed back to the hotel.

"This was nice," I said when we walked into the lobby. "Let's do it again, OK?"

"Definitely," she said.

She crossed the lobby to go to her office. I noticed she didn't speak to Miguel as he came toward me. *Odd,* I thought.

"You're up early, Senhora Keeler," he said.

"Yes. Yasmin was showing me a little of your beautiful city," I said. "I can't wait to see where Natalia will take us today. That is, if she still works here."

He looked chagrined. "Oh, yes, of course. I fire her every other day, but I couldn't really get along without her. She's very talented and she's great with the guests. They all love her."

"We certainly do," I said. "She was a great guide yesterday. That trip to Corcovado to see the statue of Christ was incredibly moving. And then she took us to this fabulous restaurant where we ate something unbelievable called a picadinho. When I asked her for the recipe, she took us back here where Luiz showed us how to cook it. She's wonderful."

"I'm glad you're pleased, senhora. I think she wants to take you to the botanical gardens today," Miguel said. "They are magnificent. But first, I thought you and your friends might like a language lesson before you go. I have persuaded Lucas to teach you some Portuguese after breakfast. Does that sound good?"

"Sounds fantastic, Senhor Ortega," I said. "I want to learn some phrases and words in your language. Thank you. I'll go tell the others."

"They're in the dining room having break-fast," he said. "They've been wondering where you were."

I walked into the elegant dining room where my friends were eating and talking all at once, the way they always do.

"Good morning, Hoofers," I said. "What's new?"

"Pat!" Mary Louise said. "What were you doing up so early?"

"Couldn't sleep," I said. "I went for a walk with Yasmin."

Four sets of ears perked up. I was immediately the center of attention.

"Tell us!" Gini said. "What did the beautiful and mysterious accountant have to say?"

I told them about our conversation, and of course Gini fastened on her statement that you make your life happen the way you want it to happen.

"What do you think she meant by that?" she asked.

"You should know, Gini," I said. "You're always doing that yourself. She's in charge of her life. But I was surprised to find out that she definitely doesn't like Lucas. I thought they were a pair when we saw them at the beach, but she says he's too negative."

"I don't know why anybody would want that old grouch anyway," Gini said. "I haven't seen him smile once."

"Well, he's going to give us a language lesson this morning," I said, and then couldn't help laughing at the expression on Gini's face. Total rejection.

"You're kidding," she said. "He'll be a laugh a minute. I thought he was a bartender and a guide. Who knew he was a language teacher too?"

"He probably gets a little extra money for doing this," I said. "He's always complaining that he doesn't get enough as a guide."

"Nothing like an unwilling, grouchy language teacher," Gini said.

"You don't have to participate, Gini," I said. "Natalia is taking us to the botanical gardens later, but this sounds like something I really would like to do. I don't know any Portuguese at all. Anybody else interested?"

There were nods and yeses all around. Gini shrugged. "I guess," she said. "Why not?"

"Where and when, Pat?" Tina asked.

"Right here. Right now. You don't even have to move. Just tell Miguel 'yes' and Lucas will appear."

Tina left the table to find Miguel, and within five minutes, Lucas joined us at our table. Just him and his iPad.

"Good morning, ladies," he said, still unsmiling. "I understand you would like to learn a few words in our language." He did not sound at all happy at this idea.

"Hey there, Lucas," Gini said. "You're going to teach us some Portuguese?"

"Yes," he said, typing something on his iPad.

He held it up. "This is how I would greet you in Portuguese this morning," he said.

He had written *"Bom dia."*

"Bom dia?" Gini said, pronouncing it "Bom dee-ah."

"No, no," Lucas said impatiently. "You must say 'Bong deer.' "

"Bong deer," Gini said. "Sounds like something you'd smoke a deer in."

We couldn't help laughing. It was such a tension breaker. This man seemed so gloomily serious.

Lucas glared at her. "If you don't want to learn our language," he said, "we don't have to continue with this. If you're going to make fun of . . ."

"No, no, Lucas," Gini said. "I'm sorry. I'll be good. Go ahead. What else do you have?"

Lucas wrote something else on his iPad and held it up.

" '*Boa tarde,*' pronounced 'boah tard' means—can you guess?"

"My snake is late?" Janice said. Tina poked her and frowned.

"Does it mean 'good afternoon'?" Tina asked, trying to soothe Lucas into a good mood with her friendly voice and smiling face. Wherever we go, I'm always grateful that Tina is our spokesperson. She has a way of making everything all right no matter what kind of nutty things the rest of us do or say.

"It does," he said, frowning at Janice. "Perhaps you will have better luck with *boa noite,*" which he pronounced "boah no-ee-te."

"Must be 'good night,' " Janice said, behaving herself.

"Or 'good evening,'" Lucas said, somewhat mollified. It's hard to stay mad at Janice. He really didn't want to be here, though. Janice or no Janice. I could have done without him, too, thank you very much, but I tried to be a credit to Tina.

"How do you say 'thank you,' and 'you're welcome'?" I asked.

Lucas almost looked pleased for a minute. "For 'thank you,' you say *'obrigada'* if you're a woman or *'obrigado'* if you're a man." He pronounced them "oobreegadah" and "oobreegado." "Then for 'you're welcome' you would say *'de nada,'* not pronounced the Spanish way—'day nah-dah'—but the Portuguese way—'chee-nah-dah.' Would you like to know how to say 'please?'"

"Yes, please," our polite Mary Louise said.

"You say *'por favor,'* pronounced 'porh favohr.'" He wrote it down on his iPad.

"That is like Spanish, isn't it, Lucas?" I asked.

"Yes, senhora," he said. He wrote something else on his pad and held it up. "This is how you say, 'I'm sorry,' in Portuguese. *Desculpe.'"* He pronounced it "des-cool-peh". "What else would you like to know?"

"I'd like to know how to say something I need in every language," Gini said, "which is 'I don't understand.'"

Lucas gave her his version of a smile. "In Brazil, you would say, *'nao entendo.'"*

Gini repeated his pronunciation. "Naw en-tehn-doo. Is that right?"

"Very good, senhora," Lucas said.

"I have one for you, Lucas," I said. "I want to say, 'How do you say that in Portuguese?'"

"You would say *'Como se diz em portugues?'* Try it, senhora."

I came as close as I could to imitating his pronunciation. "'Coo-mo seh deesh en poor-too-gaysh?' Is that right?"

"It's close enough," he said. "People will know what you're saying. And if you want to ask 'Do you speak English?' you say, *'Voce fala ingles?'* Can you say that?"

I did better with this one. "'Vo-ceh faleh en-glehsh?'"

"Very good, senhora." He glanced toward the entrance to the dining room. "I see Natalia is coming to take you away to the botanical gardens. We will conclude our lessons in Portuguese with the word for 'good-bye.' Does anyone know how to say that?'

"I think I heard someone say *'Adeus,'*" I said. "Which would make sense, since it's like a*diós* or a*dieu.* Is that right?"

"That's the formal way of saying 'good-bye,'" he said. "But people don't really say that unless they're saying good-bye forever. Most of the time, we just say *'tchau.'* It's like *'ciao'* in Italian and it's pronounced the same way. It just means 'See you later'—same as in Italian. Or you could say *'ate mais.'* Same thing." He stopped and looked around.

"That concludes our language lesson for today. *Tchau.*" He made a small bow. "Feel free to ask me any questions you might have while you're here at the Copacabana."

He nodded to Natalia as she joined us.

"*Bom dia,* Natalia," Gini said, managing to keep a straight face while saying "bong."

"And a very *bom dia* to you, too, Hoofers," Natalia said, bubbling up to us, fresh as a new day, adorable in a white cotton shirt and leggings. She wore a turquoise necklace and matching earrings and I found her irresistible. She naturally turned on the tease when she saw me looking at her.

"Miss me, Pat?" she said.

"You're very bad," I said, shaking my finger at her.

"Actually, I'm very good," she said, smiling a wicked smile.

"I understand you're taking us to the botanical gardens today, Natalia," Tina said. She likes my Denise a lot, and she wasn't going to let this wild little flirt distract me from my true love.

"Yes, yes, yes, Tina," she said. "Come—Ramon is waiting for us."

Pat's Tip for Traveling with Friends: Don't try to compete with that friend who packs everything in one small bag for a week's vacation. Take a big bag.

Chapter Eight

Come to the Garden of Eden

"Wait till you see this botanical garden," Natalia said, as Ramon drove away from the hotel. "I think it must be the most beautiful one in the world, though of course I haven't seen them all. It covers three hundred and thirty-eight acres, full of the most beautiful flowers and plants and trees you've ever seen. Orchids—purple and white and every color. Some flowers that look like candy. And everywhere there are birds you won't see in New Jersey. And monkeys jumping around from tree to tree. Everywhere you look there's something delightful. I can't wait to show it to you."

It was hard not to feel Natalia's enthusiasm and joy as she described the Jardim Botânico to us. I looked it up. That's what it's called in Portuguese.

"It was the dream of a Portuguese king called Joao VI when he came to live in Brazil in 1808," Natalia continued. "There are over 8,000 different kinds of flowers in this garden. Can you imagine! It's the most peaceful corner in the whole city. There are so many places where you can just sit down in the stillness and breathe in the quiet. You can see the statue of Christ on Corcovado from almost everywhere in the garden. Actually you can see him from any spot in the city."

I was hooked, and I could tell from the look on the faces of my friends that they were too. Especially Mary Louise. She had a lovely garden in back of her house in New Jersey. She actually enjoyed all the planting and weeding and hard work that is necessary to make things grow. I never had the patience to do all that, but Denise does, and she's turned our yard into a place of beauty. Azaleas, forsythias, and magnolia blossoms in the spring. Roses in the summertime. Asters in all different colors in the fall.

I don't know how I got along before I found Denise. She makes every part of my life better. And I adore her son, David. I loved him right away when he came to live with us because the first thing he did was to run to my cat, Eliza, and pat her. He's the one who makes sure her bowl is full of food she loves, and that she always has fresh water. He empties her litter box. And best of all, she cuddles up next to him wherever he is and purrs so loudly you can hear her in the next room. Cats always know a good person when they meet one. Or at least the person most likely to spoil them.

When Ramon pulled up to the elaborate gated entrance to the garden, we piled out. "Why don't you wander through the gardens on your own," Natalia said. "I'll meet you at the Café Botânica in an hour. You don't want me yammering at you in such a peaceful environment. We'll have some lunch and then I'll take you to the top of Sugar Loaf Mountain on one of those cable cars. It's another beautiful view of the city. How does that sound?"

I felt a little guilty. I didn't want Natalia to leave, because things are always more fun when she's around, but her plan made sense. Actually, I welcomed the chance to roam about this flower-filled paradise on my own. I didn't want to talk to anyone, not even my friends. Much as I love them, I'm glad we're not joined at the hip. We each have our own interests, our own lives, when we're not dancing together.

"What do you say, Hoofers?" Tina asked, echoing my thought. "Shall we each explore this garden separately and meet at the café in an hour?"

We all agreed. I set out to walk across the little red footbridge that led to the Japanese garden. The minute I crossed that bridge, I was in another world. There was a small pond with huge water lilies floating in it, a small gazebo with benches inside, and along the path there were flowers I had never seen before. Bright red blossoms that looked like lots of tiny candies bunched together with a spray of yellow fronds popping out of the top. The sign said they were called *combretum reticulatum* and were from Africa. Farther on there were more red flowers shaped like lobster claws, called *heliconia latispatha.*

Somehow they belonged here in this Japanese garden. It seemed like a place where surprises happened when you least expected them. For instance, in the middle of a patch of soft green leaves was a red flower that looked like a large wax rose. The sign said it was called a torch ginger, a red ginger lily, a philippine wax flower, or a *rose de porcelaine.* It was from Indonesia.

I found a small bench tucked away behind the gazebo and sat down to half meditate, half figure out what was happening here in Rio. I closed my eyes and let my thoughts come and go without trying to examine them very closely.

I started meditating about five years ago. It's one of the great blessings in my life. It seems to clear out all the annoying anxieties and bothersome stuff that accumulates during a normal day, and leaves me with what matters. It doesn't always work, of course, but most of the time it does.

This seemed like the ideal place to meditate and clear my mind of all the theories I had collected about who killed Maria. There was Lucas who was sick of paying alimony to his ex-wife. And Sumiko, Ortega's wife, who didn't want Maria to take her husband away from her. There was the doctor—Souza, I think his name was—who might or might not have supplied the anesthetic that killed her. Maybe it was Miguel Ortega, the manager, who was interested in someone else. Maybe he wanted Natalia. Maybe he and Natalia conspired to steal the anesthetic and kill Maria so they could run off together. Actually, I could not bear to think of my Natalia as a murderess. And there was Yasmin, my accountant friend. Maybe she wanted Lucas to spend his money on her instead of paying alimony to Maria. Too many maybes. I let it all go. Cleared my mind of all this stuff and tried to return to no thoughts at all.

I concentrated on my mantra, which was *om-tiddly-om*. Well, you could make up your own. I didn't want anything ordinary. This not only emptied my mind but made me smile while I was doing it. Not a sound interrupted my reverie. I thought there would be other people bustling about this forestlike garden, but Natalia must have picked a nonbusy time to come here.

After a while, I realized I only had an hour to spend in this Eden, so I reluctantly left my lovely haven and walked along a stone path through tall palm trees and huge bamboos. Everything was carefully tended and cared for. I walked along until I came to another water lily pond. This one was full of the enormous white lilies called Victoria Regia, which are the biggest water lilies I've ever seen. Next to this pond was a little hut that was labeled REPLICA OF AN AMAZON FISH-

ERMAN'S HUT. It was a humble shack, but the best part was a sculpture of a man in fisherman's clothes sitting on the bank of the pond fishing. Nice touch, I thought.

Next I came to a large building called the orchid conservatory, which claimed to house 2000 species of orchids. I went in and was overwhelmed by the beauty of hundreds and hundreds of orchids, some in a white-columned gazebo, some all around it, in purples and whites and pinks—every variation of orchids you could find. I took some pictures with my iPhone so I could look again at all this beauty on some dreary day back in New Jersey.

Time was getting short, so I walked a little faster until I came to an iron structure called the Fountain of the Muses, with the four muses of music, art, poetry, and science carved on it. Science? There was a muse of science? Who knew? The spray from the cool water coming out of the fountain was refreshing. It was a really hot day, and I welcomed the cold mist.

I realized it was time to head toward the Café Botânica and consulted the map on my iPhone to find my way. When I arrived, my friends were already there talking to Natalia and eating sandwiches.

"Here she comes, Miss America,'" Natalia sang as I walked toward the table in this outdoor restaurant. I bowed and did a pageant-type walk to join my friends.

"Where did you go?" Janice asked. "We didn't see you anywhere."

"I meditated a while in the Japanese garden," I said. "It was heaven. And I went to the orchid conservatory, which was awesome. And there was a little hut with a fisherman. It was incredible. I wish we had more time here. Where did you guys go?"

"Did you know there's a museum of carnivorous plants in this garden?" Gini asked.

"Only you would find a place full of plants that eat things!" I said. "What do they eat?"

"Mostly insects. But some of them eat frogs and even mice. You should go there, Pat. It's fascinating."

"How do they catch the things they're going to eat?" Janice asked.

"They have long skinny arms that reach out and grab flies right out of the air," Gini said. She loves to tell Janice totally outrageous things that aren't true because she knows Janice will play along with her.

"Get out of here!" Janice said.

"Oh, Janice, don't believe that!" Tina said. "How do they catch them, Gini—really?"

"Well, see, they have all different ways," Gini said. "Some of them, like Venus flytraps, sort of lie in wait for their unsuspecting prey, like insects or frogs or even mice. They're flowers, but they look like open jaws with teeth. When the bug or mouse touches two of the flytrap's hairs, the plant shuts up around them and slowly, slowly eats them. Yum."

"Gini!" Mary Louise said. "We're eating lunch!"

"No mice or frogs on the menu, though,

Weezie," Gini said. "Don't worry." She took a bite of her ham and cheese misto. "This is so good."

"If you're through ruining our appetites, Gini," I said, "I think I'll have what you're having. Looks good." I motioned to the waiter, and he went off to get my sandwich.

"I *have* to tell you about nepenthes," Gini said. "They look like beautiful pitchers and they're mainly found in Australia and Asia. They have this sweet-smelling liquid inside them that attracts insects or little mice, who fall into the plant and are devoured." She licked her lips and made slurping noises in Janice's direction.

"You are the most disgusting person I've ever met," Janice said, moving her chair farther away from Gini.

"Do you lovely ladies always have such delightful lunch table conversations?" Natalia asked.

"When Gini is with us, we usually do," Tina said. "Didn't any of you discover anything in the gardens that we can actually talk about?"

"I saw some of the most beautiful birds I've ever seen," Mary Louise said. "There's nothing like them at home. There was a seven-colored tanager with a turquoise head, a blue vest, an orange back, and—he was amazing. There was a blue finch with a yellow beak. And I saw a green parakeet with a maroon belly. And a toucan with an incredibly bright orange throat—and . . ."

Natalia's phone interrupted Mary Louise's birdsong. She left the table to answer it and was back in a minute with a worried look on her face.

"Sorry, Hoofers," she said. "We've got to get back to the hotel. There's been another murder. Sumiko."

Oh my God, I thought. It can't be. Why would anyone kill Sumiko?

I took one quick bite of my sandwich and followed the others out to the van that was waiting at the gate for us.

Nobody said anything on the way to the Copacabana. I'm sure the others all had the same sense of déjà vu I had. This was just like our trip to Giverny in France when bad news also ended our delicious lunch. One more murder like this and I'm giving up lunch.

Pat's Tip for Traveling with Friends: Keep track of who paid for what so you come out even at the end of the trip.

Chapter Nine

Have Another Bite, Honey

Senhor Pereira, the chief of police, was waiting for us when we arrived at the hotel. He was tense, not as approachable as he had been with us before.

"There has been another murder," he said. "Senhora Ortega."

"What happened to her, Senhor Pereira?" Gini asked.

"Perhaps you will allow me to ask the questions, Senhora Miller," the chief of police said sternly. "I don't want to discuss the details of this case. I'm sure you understand."

"Of course, senhor," Gini said and had the sense to shut up and step back.

"If you will follow me into the office in the back, I would like to ask you a few questions."

We followed him into Yasmin's office. As I might have expected, there was a lot of color in this room. Paintings on the wall. A red leather chair behind the desk. If you could call an office sensual, this was. Like Yasmin herself. She was already sitting there with Miguel, whose face was expressionless. He seemed numb, unable to greet us when we came in with Natalia. Dr. Souza sat next to him, glancing at him with a concerned look on his face.

The chief of police looked around the office and frowned.

"Lucas should be here too," Pereira said. "Where is he?"

"I sent for him," Yasmin said. "He should be here soon."

"We'll wait," the chief said.

No one said anything as we sat there waiting for Lucas to appear. All sorts of thoughts were running through my head. A lot of the theories that popped up in my mind in the botanical gardens had to be revised. Why would anyone want to kill Sumiko? She was a pleasant enough, little woman, certainly not annoying enough for anyone to kill her. The only person who might have wanted her out of the way was Maria, who was fooling around with her husband, but Maria was dead too.

Miguel. He wouldn't have killed his wife just so he could marry somebody else. A simple divorce would have been enough. How about Natalia? Could she have killed Maria and Sumiko? I couldn't think of any earthly reason this sparkly little singer would have wanted to kill them, but we had only known her for two days.

What about Yasmin? She might have wanted to kill Maria because of Lucas, although that certainly seemed unlikely. She said she didn't even like him. But why would she kill Sumiko? None of it made any sense, but I was sure the police chief would figure it out. I liked him. Very smart, good with people, experienced.

The office door opened, and Lucas came in, nervous, looking around the room, his gaze stopping at Yasmin, who must have given him some hidden signal because he calmed down and said to Pereira, "I'm sorry. I just got your message."

"Sit down, senhor," the chief said.

We were all silent, waiting for his next words.

"The medical examiner has removed Senhora Ortega's body from her room to the lab where they will do tests to determine what killed her. We think she may have been poisoned by the same drug that killed Maria, but we won't know until the lab has done tests. I do not want the guests in the hotel to find out about this just yet. Our technologist is running their names through the computer to see if any of them might be connected to either Maria or Sumiko in some way. Until then, I would appreciate it if all of you would try to act as normal as possible."

A low moan came out of Senhor Ortega when the chief said this.

"My apologies, Senhor Ortega," Pereira said. "I know how hard this must be for you."

Miguel wiped his eyes and nodded.

The police chief turned to us next. "You can play a big part in making things look like nothing has happened," he said. "Do you think you can dance tonight?"

"We will do our best, senhor," Tina said. Her voice was low, but her manner conveyed her confidence that we would be able to do this. I knew we could do it. That's one thing about being our age. We've all been through a lot of very difficult situations. We know how to do what we have to do without a lot of fuss.

"And you, senhora," the chief said to Natalia. "You were close to both women. Do you think you will be able to perform tonight?"

One thing I knew about Natalia by now. She might seem like a little fly-by-night flibbertigibbet, but she had nerves of steel and could do anything she had to do with grace and strength.

"You can count on me, senhor," she said.

"*Obrigado, senhora,*" he said, bowing. "You may all go now, but I will want to talk to you separately later on after we find out exactly how Senhora Ortega died." He turned to look at the doctor. "Dr. Souza, may I have a word with you privately?"

The chief motioned for the rest of us to leave and closed the door after we were gone.

"Wonder what that's all about," Gini said as we returned to the lobby. "He must suspect the doctor if he asked to speak to him alone. Especially if Sumiko died from the same anesthetic that Maria did."

"We don't know that, Gini," Tina said.

"I don't care what anyone says," Natalia said. "I don't trust that doctor."

"Neither do I," Yasmin said.

"Why not?" Gini asked.

Yeah, I thought, *why not?* What's wrong with that good-looking doctor? Aside from the fact that he was an anesthesiologist and Maria and maybe Sumiko died from being injected with an anesthetic, of course.

"Well," Natalia said, looking around to make sure the doctor was still in the office with Pereira, "I read about another doctor—actually he was from New Jersey—who was an anesthesiologist convicted of killing his wife with this anesthetic that disappears from the body. You know—that succinylcholine chloride I told you about. The police were sure he killed her but they couldn't prove it because it looked like his wife had died of a heart attack. There was no trace of any poison in her body. The medical examiner, though, was a brilliant man who managed to find traces of this anesthetic in her brain and liver. I think he puréed her brain or something."

"Ewwww," Janice said.

"It turned out the doctor killed his wife because he had a heart condition and was living on a disability income," Natalia continued. "That wasn't enough for him though. He wanted more money so he took out a large insurance policy on his wife and killed her. His lawyer, F. Lee Bailey—"

"F. Lee Bailey," Gini said. "He had F. Lee Bailey as his lawyer? Wow! He's awesome."

"Yeah, wow," Natalia said. "He was sure he was home-free with Bailey as his lawyer and an anesthetic that couldn't be detected. But a smart prosecutor and an even smarter medical examiner got him convicted."

"What a story," Gini said. "But you're not saying Ortega murdered his wife to get insurance money, are you? Or that Dr. Souza helped him by supplying the anesthetic?"

"No, no," Natalia said. "But I'm sure Souza is involved in this somehow. He certainly had easy access to that drug."

"It's all just speculation at this point," Tina said. "What do you say we practice the bossa nova that we're doing tonight. I think we need a change of scene—and a change of subject. Come on. The dance floor is clear. The band is over there tootling around. Let's ask them to play. Want to sing with us, Natalia?"

"You bet," she said.

Tina was right. I was relieved to get off the subject of murder. I could see the others were too.

Natalia asked the band to play "Blame It on the Bossa Nova," and we swung into the dance, which starts off with a waltz step, one-two-three-four, then back two steps and cross one foot in back of the other. She sang the lyrics in her sexy, very Brazilian style as we danced.

We were really getting into it, moving our bodies, dancing faster with a lot of hip moving when a few of the guests at the hotel came into the room to watch us. Gradually more and more of them came in, swaying to the music, wanting to join in.

Tina motioned for the band to stop.

"Listen, guys," she said to us. "I've got an idea. See what you think."

We gathered around her and Natalia squeezed in next to me.

"Why don't we ask the men in the audience to join us?" Tina said.

"What do you mean—join us?" Gini said, looking skeptical, the way she always does.

"They're obviously dying to dance," Tina said. "So why not let them? What do you think of this idea? Tonight, we start off dancing by ourselves the way we always do, and then when everybody is caught up in the music and the rhythm and the excitement of the bossa nova, we move into the audience, still dancing, and pick a man to dance with us on stage. They'll love it and so will we."

"What if they can't dance?" Gini asked. She always has to look for some reason a plan won't work. Come to think of it, that's usually my job.

"Let's try it out now," Tina said. "And see what happens. I'll bet they're all great dancers. This isn't New Jersey, you know."

I love New Jersey, but you could travel from Ridgewood to South Amboy and you wouldn't find a single man who could bossa nova with you, unless he was Latino or, better still, Brazilian.

"I say let's do it," Janice said. Janice is always up for everything. I knew Mary Louise would go along with whatever the rest of us wanted to do. I also knew that Gini would join us too. She had to make some kind of a fuss first. It's her nature.

"It's a great idea, Tina," Natalia said. "One small suggestion, though. To keep their wives or dates from hating you, once you've danced with their husbands, lead the men back to their tables and invite the women to dance with them too."

"Brilliant, Natalia," Tina said. "That's a truly inspired suggestion. OK, let's try doing that now—you know, asking one of the guests to dance—and see what happens."

Natalia wiggled with joy the way she always does and ran over to the band to tell them what we were going to do. I could tell from their expressions and the way they started to play with even more vigor than before that they liked the whole idea too.

We took our places on the polished floor and started bossa novaing again, putting our hearts and hips into it. We followed Tina's lead when she danced out into the group of guests and chose a tall black man, young and muscular, to come back on the floor with her. He looked first at his wife who smiled and nodded yes, and then he followed Tina and did a perfect bossa nova with her. Not a false step. The guests cheered.

Gini, our doubter, was, of course, next to join in. She approached a man who was circling in place, unable to stop moving. He wasn't particularly good-looking, but who cared? He could dance. Man, could he dance! He followed Gini onto the floor, joining Tina and her partner and swung into a bossa nova to die for.

The guests were really getting into this. They obviously loved the whole idea. Janice didn't even have to choose a partner. Dr. Souza was leaving Yasmin's office and when he saw what was going on, he put his arm around Janice and danced onto the floor with her without missing a beat. He was a natural. Handsome, sexy, somewhat mysterious, and obviously totally enthralled by Janice. Well, you know, most men are.

Mary Louise was a little shyer about dancing up to some man and asking him to bossa nova with her, but one of the women guests gave her husband a little push toward her. It didn't take more than that slight shove for him to follow Mary Louise back to the floor with the rest of us. He was just as good a dancer as the rest of them.

I was the last to choose. I'm always the last to choose because I have to weigh every alternative before I can make up my mind about anything. I know it's annoying, but what can I tell you? It's the way I am. Denise is very patient with me. While I was trying to decide which man to choose, Yasmin appeared from nowhere and guided me gently onto the dance floor. At first, I wasn't sure whether

I should do this. Do women dance with women in Rio? Probably. They seem to do everything in Rio. Anyway, the music got to me. I couldn't resist. I let Yasmin rock me into the best bossa nova I've ever done.

Nobody wanted to stop. The band kept playing more and more enthusiastically. The rest of the guests were applauding and dancing in place. Natalia jazzed up her singing and did a little bossa novaing as she sang.

Police chief Pereira came out of Yasmin's office and started to leave. His official business was done for the moment, but he was Brazilian, after all. He couldn't resist the excitement in that room. He stood on the side and clapped with the rest of the guests.

It was the most fun I've had on all our trips, I think. Maybe because it was so spontaneous, so unplanned. So unlike the rest of my life back home. I didn't want it to stop.

Tina finally motioned to us to bring our guests back to their tables. The others led their partners back to their wives or partners, who were more than ready to dance. Yasmin gave me a little hug—nothing sexy, just a friendly squeeze—and left the room.

"Time for a shower and some dinner before we do this again tonight," Tina said. "I think it went well, don't you?"

"We definitely have to do this at every performance," Janice said. "I mean, that doctor can dance!"

We all told her how much fun it had been and went to our rooms.

Back in our suite, Gini started in on me. "What's going on with you and Yasmin, Pat?" she asked. "You were really into that dance with her. I've never seen you dance like that with Denise."

"Oh, relax, Gini," I said. "It was just a friendly dance. Denise and I dance all the time. Not the bossa nova, but we dance."

"Looked like a lot more than friendly to me," Gini said.

"Get in that shower before I throw you in," I said, laughing and pushing her toward the bathroom.

We dressed in silky caftans, creamy white for Gini, pale yellow for me, and joined our other Hoofers in the dining room.

"I don't know how you can eat anything," Janice said. "We have to dance tonight, and I don't see anything light on this menu."

Tina beckoned to the waiter. "Could you help us out here?" she said. "We want something light to eat, and we're not familiar with Brazilian dishes. What's good but not heavy?"

The waiter was perfectly trained to deal with noneating Americans. He said to us in excellent English, "I can suggest several dishes that are light but delicious, senhora." He pointed to a few items on the menu and described them to us.

"There's our bobo de camarao," he said. "That's shrimp in a purée of manioc—you may know this as cassava—meal, with coconut milk and palm oil. Or you might like the chef's galin-hada. That's a chicken and rice stew, which is a little heavier than the shrimp, but still light enough, I think."

"They sound good, but still a little too much for us tonight," Tina said. "Anything else that's more like a lunch dish or a snack?"

"Ah," the waiter said. "I know just the thing. Try our pastels. They're usually just for snacks, but might be perfect for you. They're pastry shells filled with meat, or mozzarella, or chicken, little shrimp, almost anything you want. They are de-lightful and might be just what you're looking for."

"Sounds good to me," Gini said. "That's what I'll have, please."

We all ordered the pastels, and the others drank caipirinhas, while I sipped on my coconut water and lime juice. It's OK, though. I was used to it by now.

I had expected Natalia to join us, but was sur-prised to see her dining at another table with Dr. Souza. She looked stunning in a low-cut red gown—very low-cut—and was leaning toward him listening intently as he talked to her. She didn't even glance up to smile or wave at us as she usually did.

"Wonder what Natalia and the doctor are talking about over there," I said to Gini, who was sitting next to me.

"Probably figuring out whom to murder next," she said. "I think I heard your name mentioned.

In fact I'm sure I heard her say, 'I just can't stand Pat.' "

"You know you're the worst person in the world, don't you?" I said. "If they kill anybody, it should be you."

"Yes," she said. "I know. Aren't you glad you got to room with me?"

"Never again," I said. "Next time, I'm staying with Mary Louise. She's always nice to me." I didn't really mean it, of course. I love Mary Louise, but I have more fun with Gini. Always.

Gini grinned at me and I grinned back. Pals forever.

Our pastels were fantastic.

We lingered over coffee and then went back to our rooms to dress for our bossa nova that night.

Pat's Tip for Traveling with Friends: Above all, stay flexible! Nothing is written in stone.

Chapter Ten

And When She Passes By . . .

I was really looking forward to our performance this evening more than usual because of our plan to dance with guests as we had that afternoon. Brazilians seem like they were born to dance, that they were really happiest when there was music playing they could move to. They were not like any other people we had performed for in our checkered careers as dancers/murder solvers. I could not imagine Russian men, for instance, whirling us off our feet. They seemed much too earthbound.

We changed into red halter tops with skirts that looked like rows of multicolored flowers sewn together. The flowers rustled as we danced and accentuated the whole mood of the bossa nova.

The room was full when we entered. Everyone seated at the tables cheered and hurrahed as we took our places on the dance floor. The band swung into a lively version of "The Girl from Ipanema." We bossa novaed back and forth, rustling our flowers, really getting our hips into the action, clicking our fingers and smiling at the guests who, one by one, as the music accelerated, moved in their chairs at first and then stood up and swayed along with us or danced in place, obviously loving our act.

This was the reason I wouldn't give up our dancing for anything. It was the total opposite of what I did every day at home—counseling people with problems. On this dance floor, there were no problems, only sheer joy and exhilaration.

Tina broke away from our group and motioned to us to follow her out into the audience. When the guests saw us choosing a man to lead back to the floor, they clapped and cheered. Almost every man there was eager to be on that floor with us. The men we picked did the bossa nova as enthusiastically as if they had been dancing with us all their lives. No one faltered, not even one step. They were there! I mean they were a part of our act. I wanted to take them all home with me. Just to dance with, you understand.

The band reacted with the same excitement

they had shown in the rehearsal in the afternoon. Natalia sang her little heart out. She *was* the girl from Ipanema. Believe me, you would have gone aaaahhh if you had heard Natalia that night and if you had seen us dancing with Brazilian men we had never met before. Our bodies came close, moved away from each other, circled, spun, as if we had done this all our lives.

At the end of the song, we guided our partners back to their wives or lovers or whoever they were with, and the couples kept on dancing after we stopped. It was the best.

We Hoofers went back on the floor and bowed and the guests paused long enough to applaud us with cheers and cries of "More, more, more."

We rustled our skirts and as the band played a new song, we started to dance the carioca. We flashed our legs, wiggled our hips, and danced even faster until I thought I would melt. The room was really warm from all the people dancing there, and we had been moving without stopping for about an hour. When we came to the end of the dance, and the guests were cheering, Natalia ran up to us when she had finished her song, kicked off her shoes, and said, "I dare you!"

What was this imp of a girl about to do now? We watched her run to the pool off the room where we danced, dive into the water, still wearing the gown she had performed in. I couldn't resist her and neither could my wild and crazy Hoofer friends. We could never do anything like this in New Jersey. In seconds we threw off our shoes and our flowery skirts and dove into the pool in our tops and tights. Nothing has ever felt as good as that cool, clear, refreshing water. We were laughing and splashing and ruining our silk blouses, but we didn't care.

Some of the guests followed our example and jumped in with us. It could only happen in Brazil, I think. I swam a couple of laps lazily, slowly, next to Gini and Tina. We rolled over on our backs, closed our eyes, and floated along, enjoying the cool water, the fun of being in a pool in Rio in our clothes. Where else could we do this?

When we had had enough, we climbed out to see Yasmin standing there with some towels.

"Brava, Hoofers," she said, handing each one of us a thick towel.

We dried ourselves off. None of us felt like going to bed. We were still too revved up from the dancing, the fun, the swim, everything.

"That cute doctor—Gabriel, his name is— you know, Dr. Souza?" Janice said. "He asked me to go to a club with him where he says everybody goes. Lots of music, lots of entertainment. Very Rio. I think I'll go. I'm not sleepy and I want to see what nightlife is like here. Anyone else want to come?"

"I don't think he really wants anyone else along, Jan," Gini said. "Besides, I want to hit the boardwalk with my camera and see if I can get some good night shots."

"Watch it, though, Gini," Natalia said, drying her hair. "It's not exactly safe out there. Especially when you're carrying an expensive camera. Why don't you wait until daylight?"

"I asked one of the band guys—the drummer—to come with me. Mateus," Gini said. "He's big and looks tough and I promised him a drink at one of those bars along the boardwalk. He won't let anything happen to me. Don't worry, Natalia. I'll be careful."

"OK, but I really mean it when I say watch it," Natalia said. "I want you alive tomorrow so I can take you to the top of Sugar Loaf since we didn't get to do that today because of Sumiko's murder."

"Sounds good, Natalia," Gini said. "See you guys tomorrow. Pat, do you want to come along?"

"I don't think so, Gini," I said. "I feel like winding down here by the pool. Maybe have another swim. I just feel lazy but not sleepy."

"See you later then," she said, and went off to dress and grab her camera and Mateus.

"I'm going upstairs to call Peter," Tina said.

Peter was the man she meant to marry when she had time between trips to other countries. They fell in love after Tina's husband, Bill, died a couple of years ago. Peter was a partner in Bill's law firm, and they had been friends for years. Before Peter divorced his wife, the two couples hung out together all the time. When Bill died of a heart attack, Peter looked after Tina, helping her with financial and legal mat-

ters, and fell in love with her. She had thought
of him as a friend for so long, it took her a while
to love him back.

"I haven't talked to him since we got here,
and I want to tell him all about it," she said. "I
think I'll skip the part about two murders. He's
always sure I'll come home dead from one of
our dancing trips. What time is it in New Jersey,
Natalia?"

"They're an hour behind us," Natalia said.
"He's probably still up."

"That's a good time to call him," Tina said.
"He'll be working on some law case. He'll be
glad to be interrupted—I hope."

"He always loves to hear from you, Tina,"
Mary Louise said. "Go ahead and call him."

"Are you going to call George?" Tina asked
her.

"Maybe later," she said. "I don't feel like it
right now. Anyway, I saw a little cat curled up in
the lobby. I think I'll go say hello."

We went our separate ways. Jan was gorgeous,
as usual, her blond hair tied back with a scarf
that matched the black and white striped silk
jacket and pants she wore to go nightclubbing
with the doctor. Gini just threw on a black sleeveless blouse and pants to be as inconspicuous as
possible while taking pictures on the boardwalk.
She covered her red hair with a Yankees baseball hat. She always brings one along wherever
she goes. She's a fierce Yankees fan. Mateus tow-
ered over her. I was glad he was with her.

Mary Louise went upstairs to put on some

white jeans with a white top to go visit her cat, and Tina put on her nightie and climbed into bed to talk to Peter.

Before she disappeared into the night, Natalia gave me a flowery caftan, which I threw over my top and tights that were almost dry. I sat down in the Piano Bar to listen to the music and talk to anyone who turned up. It was a beautiful room, like all the others in this luxurious hotel, with exquisite flower arrangements on the tables, tall green plants in the corners, an elaborate chandelier overhead, and large upholstered chairs to sit in. The pianist smiled at me when I sat down and he segued into "The Girl from Ipanema" to welcome me. I was relaxed and not worried about anything for a change. Not even the two murders.

I spoke too soon.

"Senhora Keeler, may I join you?"

It was Lucas, Maria's ex-husband, my least favorite person in this hotel. He looked frazzled, his shirt open at the collar, his face worried and distracted. He didn't look at me, just sat down, stood up, not sure what to do.

What would he want to talk to me about? I wondered.

"Of course, Lucas. Please sit down," I said.

He ordered a liqueur from the bartender and drummed his fingers on the glass tabletop while he waited for it.

"Was there something you wanted to talk to me about, Lucas?" I asked.

His drink arrived, and he took a sip before he answered.

"Senhora," he began, not looking at me, "did Yasmin tell you anything about the finances of this hotel when you went for a walk with her the other day?"

How did he know I went for a walk with Yasmin? Word certainly gets around in this hotel.

"Of course not," I said. "We talked about Rio and the hotel and Maria's death and . . ."

"Maria," he said. The expression on his face hardened. "She was bleeding me dry."

"Why are you telling me this, Lucas?" I asked. "Is there something I can do to help?"

He hesitated, then looked at me.

"I want to get my old job back as bartender here at the hotel. It pays a lot more than being a guide, and I get tips. But Yasmin keeps telling me she has no power to get my job back. It's the main reason I'm spending time with her. She's supposed to have some influence with Miguel." He paused and looked around to make sure Yasmin wasn't nearby.

"She said I had to talk to Miguel," he continued. "When I asked Miguel to take me back, he said something vague about there not being enough money to do that. That the hotel was losing money. That's crazy. This is the most prosperous hotel in Rio. He said he only hires part-time bartenders and pays them much less than he would have to pay me."

"What makes you think I can change his mind?" I asked.

"He likes you and the other Hoofers. If you ask him to bring me back because you think I would do a good job—and I would—he'd listen to you."

"I'd like to help you, Lucas, but you're giving me way more credit than I deserve. Senhor Ortega wouldn't care whether we Hoofers liked you or not. He's made up his mind. Why did he fire you anyway?"

"Maria demanded it. She didn't like seeing me here at the hotel. She wanted me to get a better paying job so I could give her more money."

Whenever he mentioned Maria, the pure hatred he felt for her showed plainly on his face.

"You really resented Maria, didn't you?" I asked.

"Yes, I did," he said fiercely. "But I didn't kill her, if that's what you're insinuating."

"I'm sure you didn't," I said in as soothing a tone as I could dredge up. I wasn't at all sure he didn't.

"It's a relief not to have to give her all my money anymore, but I'm not making any money as a guide. I need to come back here to work."

"I'll see what I can do," I said. "But don't expect me to be much help."

"All I ask is that you try," he said. He got up and held out his hand. "Thank you, senhora."

He walked away, and my relaxed mood went with him. How the heck could I persuade the manager of this hotel to rehire someone he didn't like? I decided to call it a night. Walking across the lobby toward the elevators, I heard one of my favorite sounds in the world.

"Meow."

I looked toward the bellman's luggage room and saw Mary Louise sitting on a large suitcase and holding the tortoiseshell cat who lived at the hotel. She looked just like my own cat, Eliza, whom I missed whenever we went on one of these trips. Mary Louise was petting her, and the kitty seemed to love the attention.

"Oh, Mary Louise, she's beautiful. May I hold her?"

"Of course. That's why I brought her over here. She has the same sweet disposition your Eliza has. Here, take her. Be gentle. She looks like a nursing mom."

I opened my arms, and this little cat cuddled up against me as if we had known each other all our lives. I patted her soft fur, and she purred to say thank you.

"What's her name?" I asked.

"Teodora," she said. "I Googled it. It means God's gift."

I put my face down on top of this velvety creature's head and Teodora purred even louder. I smiled at Mary Louise.

"You always come up with the best things," I said to her. "How did you know I needed a cat just now?"

"We always need a cat," she said. "They're God's way of saying, 'Calm down. Nothing is worth getting upset about. As long as you have food, water and a litter box, you're fine.'"

I laughed, and Teodora looked up at me, then settled in against my body. I sat down on a suitcase next to Mary Louise's so we'd both be comfy.

"As long as our little cat has a friend to love her, I think I'll go back to my room and call George," Mary Louise said. She didn't look very happy about it, but she's a loyal wife to George no matter how grumpy he gets. George is a good guy, but he runs a small law firm in New Jersey, and he always seems to have more work than he can handle.

"Say hello to him for me," I said.

She gave one last pat to the little cat and went off to her room. As I sat there, enjoying the chance to relax with a feline friend, the hotel manager spotted me and came into the luggage room.

"Have you joined our staff, Senhora Keeler?" he said with a smile. "Ah, I see you have made friends with our Teodora." Miguel leaned over to pat her.

"I have a tortoiseshell cat at home just like her," I said. "I miss her a lot, so I'm grateful to have a few minutes with your cat."

"She often comes and curls up on a corner of my desk," he said. "Sumiko didn't like cats, so Teodora adopted me."

"Does Teodora have a nest of kittens somewhere?" I asked. "She seems to be a recent mother."

"Yes, she is," Miguel confirmed. "But she likes

her privacy. No one has been able to figure out where she's hidden her babies. We've tried to follow her, but she's too clever for us. So we just give her a little extra food and let her keep them secret."

This was a warmer side of Senhor Ortega than I had seen before. It seemed a good time to bring up the subject of Lucas.

"Senhor Ortega," I said. "Lucas talked to me a little while ago, and . . ."

He frowned. "I hope he didn't bother you, Senhora Keeler."

"Oh, no, no. Not at all. He asked me if I would talk to you and recommend him for the bartenders' job again. I told him it was your decision entirely, but I promised I would ask you."

"He had no right to ask you to do that," he said in such a loud voice that Teodora started at the sudden noise and jumped out of my arms. She ran back toward the lobby. Suddenly feeling ridiculous in the luggage room, I got up to follow her. Miguel took my elbow and steered me to a pair of comfortable chairs in an alcove. We sat, and he leaned forward to speak to me in a low tone.

"I am not going to rehire him. I told him we could not afford to pay him a full-time bartender's fee. Besides, I don't want him around after the way he treated Maria."

"His resentment toward her because of the alimony, you mean," I said.

"Not just that. He used to hit her when they were married. And he cheated on her all the time. I don't like him, and I'm not going to re-hire him. I know you were just being kind, sen-hora, but he is not a good person. I don't like to see you pestered by him."

"I said I'd try," I said. "And I've done that." I waited a minute and then said hesitantly, "May I ask how the hotel is doing—I mean financially? I know it's none of my business, but I'm just cu-rious. You seem to have so many guests, and this is one of the most expensive hotels in Rio. I wouldn't have thought you'd have any money problems."

He didn't answer right away. He stood up and paced back and forth as if trying to decide how much he should tell me.

Finally, he said, "Senhora, it's the high ex-pense of running this hotel. It's called a palace for good reason. Everything has to be the very best quality. I ask Yasmin all the time why we are having financial problems, and she points out the high salaries of all the people who work here, the maintenance fees to keep everything in per-fect shape, the expensive food we serve. The chef makes a lot of money. It all adds up. When Maria was alive, she used to question me about this also. She used to tell me to raise the price of the rooms, and I did this several times. But still we didn't seem to clear much every month."

"I think it's a common problem everywhere today," I said. "Even so, I would have thought the Copacabana would be making tons of money. It's one of the most beautiful hotels I've ever stayed in."

He took a deep breath and sighed. "I would have thought so too."

"At any rate," he continued, "it's not anything for you to worry about. I'll tell Lucas not to bother you again."

He stood and went back to the Piano Bar to make sure everything was going well. I settled back in my chair and closed my eyes. So peaceful. Such a beautiful place to be. I didn't want to move.

The next thing I knew, someone was gently shaking my shoulder.

"Time for bed, sleepyhead," Yasmin said. "You don't want to sleep down here all night."

I opened my eyes and smiled at her, then stretched and sat up.

"Thanks, Yasmin," I said. "I really would have slept here until morning if you hadn't wakened me."

She helped me to my feet. "I saw you talking to Miguel before," she said. "He seemed angry. What was the problem?"

"Oh, nothing really," I said. "He was angry because Lucas asked me to get his job back as bartender. He didn't want me to be annoyed by him. He seems to be set against hiring Lucas again, though, so I didn't pursue the subject any further."

"That was it? That was—all you talked about?" she asked.

For some reason I didn't tell her about the rest of it. I didn't want to talk to her about his anxiety about the financial state of the hotel. I'm not sure why I didn't. Some instinct made me keep it to myself.

"That was it," I said. "Good night, Yasmin. Think I'll turn in." I pushed the elevator button.

"See you tomorrow, Pat," she said and headed for the piano bar.

Gini was still out when I got back to our room. I fell asleep within minutes of getting into bed.

Pat's Tip for Traveling with Friends: Discuss who will do the driving ahead of time. If you both hate driving, hire someone.

Chapter Eleven

Did Somebody Call a Doctor?

We met for a light breakfast the next morning and compared notes about our late-night adventures. The most intriguing was Janice's nightclubbing with the doctor. Our questions poured out all at once: What was he like? What did they do? Did she like him? Where did they go? Was she going to see him again? All in a rush.

"He hardly talked about his personal life at all," Janice said. "That usually means the guy's married. He didn't mention anything about a wife, but I don't think I'll go out with him again. Just a feeling."

"What *did* he talk about?" Gini asked.

"Mostly about Rio and how beautiful it is and all the things we should see while we're here. And then, just as if we had been going out for months, he asked me if I would like to go to his cabana on the beach."

"What!" I couldn't help but yell. "What do you mean, his 'cabana on the beach'? Weren't you in a nightclub?"

"Oh, yes—and it was great. Fantastic music, a great show, and we danced. But to him it seemed like a natural thing to ask me to fool around with him in his cabana. I mean, naturally, I assumed that was what he had in mind. He didn't actually say that, but his attitude was, 'I can always ask. What can I lose?' He said we could go for a swim. That he had extra bathing suits there—and then—"

"And then, what?" I couldn't help it. How could he be so casual about luring some woman he had just met to his cabana, helping her change into a bathing suit, which, as we all knew, was a couple of tiny pieces of material, and then doing who knows what? Well, I did know what.

"Cool it, Pat," Janice said, patting my hand. "I didn't go to the cabana. We just danced and walked along the boardwalk for a while, and then he brought me back here. He asked to take me somewhere tonight."

"Are you going?" Tina asked.

"I don't think so," she said. "Depends on what else turns up. I don't really like the idea that he's probably married. I've had enough of married men, thank you."

"Did the doctor say anything about the two murders or who might have killed Maria and Sumiko?" Gini asked.

"No, every time I tried to bring the subject up, he gave me some vague, one-word answer and talked about something else. He definitely didn't want to discuss it."

"Maria and possibly Sumiko died of some weird anesthetic that disappears once it's in somebody's body, and he's an anesthesiologist," Gini said. "Doesn't that seem a little suspicious to you?"

"Well, of course, Madame Prosecutor," Janice said. "But what was I going to say? 'Pardon me, sir, did you murder Maria and Sumiko with your weird anesthetic?' Come on, Gini."

"Well, you can't tell me he didn't have something to do with those deaths."

Our favorite guide joined us at the table and chimed in. "He's not a murderer, guys," Natalia said. "I've known him a long time. We had an affair once. And you're right, Janice. He is married. He has three teenaged children. He never, ever, talks about his family."

"I'm glad you told me," Janice said. "I was pretty sure he was married. He was so secretive. That's my last date with him."

"How about a day away from this hotel and all this talk of murder and cheating husbands?" Natalia said. "Are you ready to go to the top of Sugar Loaf Mountain?"

"Lead on," Gini said. "It's supposed to be incredible."

"You'll get some great shots up there, Gini," Natalia said. "It's the best view in the city. I think it's even better than Corcovado."

She took us out to the van that was waiting for us. Ramon was our driver again. He smiled a welcome as we got in.

"To Sugar Loaf, please, Ramon," Natalia said.

We drove through the busy streets to Praia Vermelha, which Natalia told us meant Red Beach, where we would find the cable car that would take us up to the top of Sugar Loaf.

My heart stopped for a moment when I saw the cable cars, which were entirely made of glass. I knew riding in one of them would make me feel as if I were actually hanging in space. I am so leery of heights. My stomach turns over a couple of times when I am in a high place. It's because when I was a little girl I went to the top of the Woolworth building in New York and some idiot—I think he was the elevator man—as a joke, pretended to throw me over the side. I can still feel that absolute terror inside as he swung me up and almost out into the air. I screamed, and I still feel like screaming when I look out into space from a high tower or place.

But when we actually stepped into the cable car here in Rio, I felt safe because there were people all around us. The cars hold sixty-five passengers, and there were close to that number on this sunny morning. Natalia, who picks up on everything, noticed my nervousness and stood next to me. I knew she was talking a lot to distract me.

"The car stops first at Morro da Urca," she said. "It's not very high. Then we take another cable car to the top, which is called Pão de Acu-car, or Sugar Loaf Mountain. There is an amazing view of the city, and there are railings everywhere to hold on to. You can walk around up there on trails through trees and shrubs."

She lowered her voice and said to me, "You OK, Pat?"

"I will be," I said. "Thanks, Natalia. How did you know?"

"I've done this a few thousand times before. I recognize that look. Lots of people are that way about heights. But don't worry—you won't get the feeling that you're suspended in space up there. It's very tourist-friendly."

We changed cars at the first mountain and arrived at the top of Sugar Loaf before I had a chance to be nervous. We stepped out onto a tree-filled aerie. The first thing I saw was the statue of Christ far off in the distance at the top of Corcovado. I felt like His outstretched arms were waving to me, reassuring me that I was safe. I relaxed.

As usual, we five separated to explore the mountain on our own. I walked over to the rail to get that part of it over with before moving inland to walk up the path. Janice joined me.

"Want to walk along that trail?" Janice asked.

"Love to," I said. "I thought I should look at the view of Rio first."

It was really a spectacular sight. Far below us we could see the city full of white buildings spread out. We could see the beaches, white next to the blue water. The curved Copacabana Beach. The Ipanema Beach. The ocean. Rock formations and mini forests were dotted among the buildings all through the city. My fear of heights calmed down a little as I absorbed the view of this magnificent city.

After a couple of minutes, Janice grabbed my arm and led me to a trail winding through the trees that lined the path.

It was cooler here, the leafy branches shading us from the sun.

We walked along in silence for a while, admiring the greenery, smiling at the monkeys who jumped from tree to tree, enjoying the quiet. After a while, I sensed that Janice wanted to talk but was hesitating.

"What is it, Jan?" I asked. "Is something the matter?"

"You certainly picked the right career, Pat," she said, sounding relieved. "Yes, there is something I need to talk to you about. It's probably nothing, but I wanted to try it out on you before I said anything to the others. As I said, it's probably nothing."

"I won't say a word to anyone until you say it's OK," I said.

She waited, pointed to a bench along the side of the path, and we sat down.

"It's something Dr. Souza—Gabriel—said when we went out last night. It seemed so strange, Pat, and he changed the subject right after he said it."

"Sounds serious, Jan. What did he say?"

She pushed back her hair and continued. "I had just asked him about Sumiko, Ortega's wife, because I knew he had been having an affair with her. Everyone knew it. I asked him what she was like and why someone would have wanted to kill her. He didn't say anything at first. He looked like he was trying to decide whether he should talk to me about her. Then he said, 'I think she found out something she wasn't supposed to know about the finances of the hotel.'"

Again. The finances of the hotel. "Really?" I said. "Wow. Then what did he say?"

"I asked him what she found out. He started to say something, but then decided he shouldn't be discussing this and described the food we were eating or something."

"Very interesting, Jan," I said. "You should mention this conversation to Chief Pereira. Remember when we were in Yasmin's office, he asked the rest of us to leave and kept Souza in there for some more questions. Maybe he suspects him already, and this would give him more to go on."

"Oh, I feel really funny about talking to the chief, Pat. That's why I wanted to tell you first. You're really good about doing things like that. Would you mind mentioning it to him?"

"Sure, Jan," I said. "I can do that. But he's going to want to talk to you, too, you know. You're

the one who heard him say it. Souza must know
what it was that Sumiko knew that she shouldn't
have known."

"OK. I'll go with you. You're just better at
these things than I am."

"Maybe it's my training as a counselor," I said.
"I try to separate what's real from what's not."

"I've noticed," Janice said. "You're really good
at it." She stood up. "Want to walk a little farther?"

"Sure," I said. We walked to the next observa-
tion point and leaned on the rail to look down
at Guanabara Bay below us. A few boats were
drifting along, their sails little white dots against
the blue water. Even this far up we could see hundreds of red umbrellas on the beaches below us.
They looked like polka dots on a white skirt.

I turned to Janice. "There's another mystery
at the hotel that I just found out about."

"Oh, no! Not another murder, I hope," she
exclaimed.

I laughed. "No, this is one you will like. It con-
cerns a cat and a secret nest of kittens."

Janice relaxed as I told her about Teodora
and her hidden babies.

"Think we should head back?" I asked. "Natalia said we had about an hour up here and
we've been gone awhile."

"Yeah, we'd better. I'm so glad I had a chance
to talk to you, Pat. I've been really worried about
this since I went out with him. I needed someone
to tell me I should say something."

"We'll go see the chief when we get back to

the hotel," I said. "I think it's really helpful information. He'll be grateful to you for telling him."

"I hope so," she said.

When we returned to our starting point, the rest of our gang was gathered around Natalia, who waved to us to follow her to the cable car.

When we were in the van, Natalia said, "I thought maybe you'd like to go to one of our famous flea markets here in Rio. They have everything—purses, sandals, paintings, jewelry, scarves, rugs. Want to go?"

I don't care much about shopping and neither does Gini, but it was obvious that Tina, Mary Louise, and Janice loved the idea.

"I heard about the flea markets of Rio before we came here," Mary Louise said. "I can't wait to go to one."

"One word of warning, though," Natalia said. "There are pickpockets everywhere in that market so wear your purse over your shoulder and across your chest. I know it's a pain, but I don't want anybody getting robbed on this trip."

The flea market seemed to stretch for miles. Natalia pointed to a small café and said, "Meet you there in an hour."

We separated and walked through the acres of tables. I wanted to get something for Denise so I headed for a table piled high with scarves. There were real Ferragamos and knock-off Ferragamos. Real Diors and fake Diors. And there were other designers I had never heard of, mostly because they're so expensive. But I found an actual Ferragamo in my price range that I knew Denise would love. She has dark hair and blue eyes and her skin is ivory pure. The scarf was a red and white print, an Art Deco flowery design that would be perfect with the black suit she just bought. She's in public relations and always looks fantastic. She tries to teach me about fashion, but I really don't care. I just want to look good. It doesn't matter whether I'm wearing whatever is in fashion at the moment.

I bought the scarf for Denise and looked around for my friends. Gini was photographing the shoppers. She couldn't care less about the piles of stuff on the tables. She wanted to catch the expressions of the people who bought them.

Tina and Mary Louise were checking out purses. Janice was going wild at a table full of shoes with the highest heels I've ever seen. Only Janice could get away with stilettos like that, or walk in them for that matter. I went over to see which shoes she would buy.

"Oh, Pat," she said. "I'm glad you're here. Help me choose."

She had three pairs in front of her. One was silver with an ankle strap and a thin strip across her toes, and heels that were at least six inches high. The next one was a regular black satin pump with stiltlike heels. The third was a black and beige striped pump with equally high heels. They were all stunning and would look fantastic on Jan's feet.

"Why don't you get them all?" I asked. "Every one is gorgeous."

"I can't do that," she said. "Can I?"

Jan often needs permission to do things she really wants to do. I'm always glad to give her that permission. She looked at each pair of shoes again. Picked them up, put them down, tried them on, and checked them out in the full-length mirror next to the table.

"Perfect for senhora," the lady behind the table said. She was middle-aged and wore flats.

"You really think so?" Janice said. "OK, I'll take all three pairs. Wrap 'em up, please. Who knows if I'll ever be back here again?"

I love Janice's whole attitude toward life: "If not now, when?" I envy her. I always find too many reasons not to do things I really want to do. I could blame it on my mother who always said, "Not now, dear. Later." Her shopping philosophy was: If you wait, you probably won't buy it and you'll save the money. Or I could use my counselor's training and realize I'm all grown up and don't have to abide by my mother's rules anymore. *Lots of luck with that one, Pat.*

Janice picked up her bag of shoes, and we joined Tina and Mary Louise at the purse table. Even I was tempted by these purses. I usually carry around a battered old thing because I hate the thought of spending a couple of hundred dollars on one, but these were hard to resist.

Tina was turning a light blue bag around and around, looking inside it. "What do you think,

Pat?" she said. "It's a Chanel. And half the price it would be at home. Should I get it?"

"It's really beautiful, Tina," I said. "Go ahead."

Mary Louise showed me the white leather purse she had just bought. It wasn't one of those huge bags that everyone carries now. It was a medium-sized, just-right purse for life in New Jersey with trips into New York. Mary Louise never needed any permission to buy anything. She knew what she liked, what she could afford, and what was in.

It was personal decisions she had trouble with. Was she taking too much time away from George when she went on our dancing sprees? Should she keep on seeing that nice American doctor she met in Spain for lunch in New York without telling George? Did she spend enough time with her children? I could help her with problems like that—but not with purses.

They gathered up their purchases, and we headed for the café Natalia had told us about. We grabbed Gini along the way. She was totally absorbed in her picture-taking and would have lost all sense of time. We pried her loose from her lens and led her to the café.

"One more, guys," Gini pleaded, and stopped to snap a photo of a scruffy brown dog nibbling at the cookie a friendly little boy was holding out to him.

Natalia was waiting for us at the restaurant. "How did you do, girls?" she asked. We showed her our purchases, and she made appreciative noises, especially at Jan's shoes when she saw the six-inch heels. "I love these," she said. "You have to show me where you found them when we finish, Jan."

We sat around an outdoor table so we could watch people of all stripes, colors, and shapes meander or bustle by looking for bargains. I would never go to a flea market at home, but here it seemed absolutely appropriate. And I loved the scarf I found for Denise. She always looks great in red. Actually, she looks good in every color.

The waiter gave us a menu. Natalia translated for us.

"There's a bacalhau a gomes de sá com ovos caipira, which is scrambled eggs with cod, olives, and tomatoes. Yum. Then there's my favorite: rabanada crocante com compota de maçã, which is a long way of saying French toast with apple compote and clotted cream. And finally, ladies, there's linguiça calabresa com ovos, or to you, Brazilian sausage and eggs. The rest of the stuff is heavy and more appropriate for dinner. What appeals to you?"

We ordered all three lunches so we could trade and sample each one of them.

"Are you dancing tonight?" Natalia asked.

"I think so," Tina said. "Miguel was so pleased with us last night, he asked if we would add an extra performance tonight. He'll pay us more. Want to, guys?" she asked us.

"What Latin delight are we dancing?" Gini asked.

"How about the mambo?" Tina said. "It's really fun and we can grab men out of the audience again and dance with them again. I loved doing that last night."

"No one has ever done that before," Natalia said. "And everyone loved it. I'm glad you're going to do it again. I'll give you a choice of songs later."

The food arrived, and we passed the dishes around to taste everything.

It was all delicious. We got too caught up in munching to talk much. But then Gini brought us back to the present.

"You know," she said, "we go sightseeing and flea market shopping and eating great food as if two people hadn't been murdered back at the famous hotel we're staying in. What's the matter with us?"

"Oh, Gini, leave it alone, at least until we finish our lunch," Janice said. "We didn't kill them and we don't know who did kill them—or at least we don't know for sure."

"What do you mean,'for sure'?" Gini said. "It could have been anybody. Who do you think did it?"

"Well, obviously Lucas killed Maria so he wouldn't have to pay her alimony anymore," Janice said.

"But why would he·kill Sumiko?" Gini asked. "She didn't do anything to him."

"Well, I haven't figured that part out yet," Janice said. "And I don't understand something Gabriel said. . . ." She stopped and looked at me. "Oh, I wasn't going to say anything about that until I talked to the police chief."

"Gabriel? You mean the doctor?" Gini said, almost choking on her sausage. "What did he say?"

Janice looked totally bummed out. "It's probably not important, Gini. I really don't want to talk about it."

"You can't just bring up something like that and then not finish your sentence!" Gini said. She never just lets anything drop, as you've probably noticed.

"Pat . . ." Janice said, looking frantically to me for help.

I jumped in. "It was just some reference to Sumiko and the finances of the hotel, but he didn't actually say much. I told Janice she should tell the police chief about it because it might be useful information."

"Just exactly what did he say about Sumiko and the finances of the hotel?" Gini insisted. "Come on, Jan."

"Well, I asked him about Sumiko—I knew he was going out with her—and I asked him why he thought somebody killed her. He said he thought she found out something about the financial situation of the hotel that she wasn't supposed to know. Then he changed the subject and didn't say anything more."

"There's definitely something fishy about the money at the Copacabana," I said. "I meant to tell you guys. Last night after we danced, Lucas came over to me and asked me if I knew anything about money problems in this hotel. He said he asked Yasmin to rehire him as bartender in the hotel. She said he would have to ask Ortega. When he did, Ortega said he couldn't afford to rehire him because the hotel wasn't doing very well. That sounded really weird to me. Since this is such an expensive hotel, I assumed they made tons of money."

"That's ridiculous," Natalia said. "They do make tons of money in this hotel! Lucas just makes all that stuff up to cause trouble. He's always been a troublemaker. Miguel said that he couldn't afford to rehire Lucas because he hates him. Believe me, this hotel has no money problems."

She stopped and took her phone out of her purse. "Excuse me a minute, ladies. Someone's calling me."

She listened, and her whole expression changed. "It can't be," she said. "I don't believe it. Yes, of course, Senhor Pereira, we'll return to the hotel at once."

"What is it, Natalia?" Tina said.

"You won't believe this," Natalia said, motioning to the waiter for the check. "There's been another murder."

"Who?" Gini said, putting down her fork and wiping her mouth. "Who is it this time?"

"Gabriel. Dr. Souza," Natalia said, her face pale. "They just found him."

"My God," Janice said. "How can that be? I thought he was . . ."

"The murderer?" Natalia said. "I told you he could never kill anybody. I've known him forever. He saves lives—not takes them. Come on, Hoofers, we've got to get back to the hotel."

We left the remains of our delicious lunch on the table and went out to the van where Ramon was waiting for us, his face serious.

"Back to the hotel, Ramon. There's been another murder," Natalia said.

"Oh, no, senhora," he said. "That cannot be."

We got in the car and drove back to the Copacabana, where, once again, Chief Pereira was waiting for us. Ortega and Yasmin were standing with him.

"I'm sorry to have to tell you that a third person in this hotel has been killed," he said. "Dr. Souza. He was found floating facedown in the pool this afternoon by one of the hotel maids. We got him to the hospital immediately, but it was too late. We still don't know what killed him. If any of you has anything to tell me, please do so immediately."

Janice looked at me, and I said, "I don't know how significant it is, sir, but Senhora Rogers and I have something that might be of interest."

"Please, senhora—"

I told him about Janice's conversation with the doctor the night before, and he made some notes on his iPad.

"Thank you for this information, senhora. This is very helpful. Please be available for more questions later."

He motioned to Yasmin, Ortega, and Natalia to follow him into Yasmin's office. We stood there stunned, unsure of what to do next.

"I need a drink," Gini said.

"Me too," Tina said. "Let's go in the Piano Bar and order a cosmo. I want something American."

We went into the bar, where the pianist was playing some Gershwin songs that were just right for our mood—especially when he played, "Someone to Watch Over Me." My friends ordered cosmos and I asked for a coconut water and lime drink, which I was actually beginning to like. We looked at each other in disbelief.

"I'm beginning to think we're a curse," Janice said. "Everywhere we go, people die by the carload. Maybe we should just stay home before we kill off the entire population of the world."

"Well, it won't be long before the entire population of this hotel will be gone," Gini said. "I don't get it. Who could be doing this? Maria, Sumiko, Dr. Souza. Who would want to kill all three of these people?"

"They don't really have anything in common," I said. "Maybe, just maybe, Lucas killed Maria so he wouldn't have to pay her alimony anymore, but he had no reason to kill Sumiko and Souza. And Ortega? He might have wanted his wife dead so he could fool around more, but why would he kill Souza? Who else is there?"

"There's Yasmin and Natalia," Gini said, "but why would they bump off Maria, Sumiko, and Souza? It just doesn't make sense."

"I still think it has something to do with money," I said. "There's some reason this hotel isn't making a serious profit. If we can find that out, we'll have our murderer."

"Not necessarily," Yasmin said, coming out of her conference with the chief and appearing at our table. She always seemed to pop up when we were least expecting her. "Inflation affects every business these days. The hotel merely spends more than it takes in. It's that simple. I'm the one who sees where the money goes, after all."

I still had my doubts, but I dropped the subject and invited Yasmin to join us.

"I'd love to," she said, "but I'm meeting an old friend. I'll see you later." She started to leave and then turned back and knelt at my side. I was sitting a little apart from the others, and she spoke to me in a low voice so my friends wouldn't hear.

"Pat, how would you like to come with me to an authentic *baile funk* in the favelas near here later this evening?"

"What's a *baile funk?*" I asked her.

"It's a huge street party in the heart of Rio's slums. They call them favelas. They're on a hillside near here. We just walk up there, and friends of mine will let us in. There's nothing like it. Wild music, great dancing, some pot, if you're in the mood, since you don't drink. You'll love it."

"What about my friends?" I asked. "Can they come too?"

"I'm only allowed to bring one person," she said. "See, it's mostly black people. They're the ones who live there, but I know someone who lets me in. I wanted to take you to one of these since we danced together." She put her cheek against mine and whispered in my ear, "I just want to be alone with you."

I knew I should say no, but I couldn't resist. It was too exciting a prospect to turn down. Even cautious old me couldn't refuse this chance at something different, probably illegal, definitely unlike anything I would find at home in New Jersey. I don't mean to make New Jersey sound boring. I love living there. But it sure ain't Rio!

"What time?" I asked.

"I'll pick you up about eleven," she said.

"You're on," I said.

She left and Gini, who never misses anything interesting that's going on, said, "So, what's happening with you and Yasmin?"

"Oh, nothing," I said. "She thought I might like to go to something called a *baile funk* with her after we dance tonight."

"Sounds intriguing. What's a *baile funk?*"

"Some kind of wild dance party in the favelas," I said.

"Ooh, can I come too?" she asked.

"I asked her if I could bring our whole gang, but she said no. She said she was restricted in the number of outsiders she could bring. They don't trust anybody up there." I looked at the rest of my fellow Hoofers. "Sorry, guys."

"I understand," Gini said. "Sounds intriguing. I'll wait up for you."

"I might be really late," I said, trying to discourage her. "I don't want you sitting here worrying about me until three in the morning." But Gini isn't easily discouraged.

"Like I said, I'll wait up," she said.

Miguel Ortega came into the bar after his session with the police chief. He looked distracted. He didn't seem to notice us until Tina spoke to him.

"Miguel," Tina said, "do you still want us to dance tonight? I wasn't sure. I mean, with the doctor's death and all. We'll do whatever you want."

He didn't answer her at first. His mind was miles away and he couldn't seem to concentrate on what she was saying.

"Miguel?" Tina said again.

"Oh, forgive me, Senhora Powell," he said. "What did you say?"

Tina repeated her question.

"If you can dance with all this going on," he said, "I would be most grateful."

"Of course," Tina said. "We'll do a carioca and invite the men in the audience to dance with us. That seemed to work last night."

"People were still talking about it today," Ortega said. "Please do it again tonight. Perhaps you will permit me to dance with you?" He bowed and kissed her hand. He seemed to have recovered his host persona once more.

"It would be a great pleasure, Senhor Ortega," Tina said as he left the room.

"Looks like you have a secret admirer, Tina," I said.

"Not really, Pat," she said. "That's his manager-of-the-hotel personality. Nothing to do with me."

Natalia came out of the office and joined us.

"What do you think, Natalia," Tina said. "Can you sing that carioca song tonight?"

"Been doing it all my life," she said with a wink and a shimmy.

"What did the police chief ask you?" Gini said.

Natalia's face was suddenly serious. No more fooling around. "I don't want to talk about it, Gini. He thinks because I went out with Gabriel that I knew who killed him. I haven't a clue, but don't ask me about it anymore, OK?"

Gini got it. She reached out and touched Natalia's arm. "Sorry, hon. No more questions."

"Natalia," Janice said, "I don't really want a big hotel meal tonight before we dance. Is there somewhere I can go and just get a quick bite?"

"Of course," she said. "There are a million what they call *botequin*s around here. They have mostly appetizers and stuff to drink. I'll take you to my favorite one, if you want."

"Sounds like exactly what I want," Janice said. "Anybody else?"

Tina, Mary Louise, and Gini said they would come along to the *botequin*, but I didn't need anything to eat. I just wanted to rest, dance, and then party at the *baile funk*. The thought of food made me feel a little sick.

I wandered into the lobby to find my little cat,

Teodora, but she wasn't curled up in her regular spot in the luggage room. I asked the bellman where she was and he said he hadn't seen her since the night before. I decided to go back up to my room and veg out, but just as I pushed the elevator button, Miguel Ortega called to me, "Senhora Keeler," he said. "Want to see something wonderful?"

"Oh, yes, senhor," I said. "I'm definitely in the mood for something wonderful."

"Come with me," he said, and led me into his office. There in the corner was Teodora in a basket with five little kittens playing around her. She looked totally content. One of the kittens, a little yellow tiger, was playing with Teodora's tail, while two gray tabbies stalked each other around the edges of the basket. The other two kittens were of the Heinz 57 variety, seeming to combine every color a cat could possibly have. They were snoozing and snuggling next to Teodora.

"Oh, how precious," I said. "Where did you find them?"

"I didn't," he said. "Early this morning, when I stepped off the elevator, I saw Teodora leading a parade of kittens through the lobby. I unlocked my office and she marched right in. I gave them a basket from the florist shop, and they seem quite happy here now."

"What lucky kitties," I said, giving Teodora a scratch on her ears. "You're a good mom cat, aren't you, sweetie?"

"You really love cats, senhora," Ortega said.

"I do," I said. "And Teodora looks just like my Eliza. Her kittens are beautiful."

"Do you want one of them?" he asked me.

"Oh, I'd love one," I said. "But they're too little to take with me now. I'm sure you can find a good home for them when they're older. "

This man, who had seemed so formal and unapproachable, was now my friend. First name and all. Kittens will do that.

I bent to pat Teodora on the head.

"Your children are beautiful," I said to her, and she gave a soft little purr. I stood up and shook Miguel's hand.

"Thank you for showing me these babies. *Ate logo,*" I said, pronouncing it "atay logu," hoping I had pronounced the Portuguese words for "see you later" correctly.

"*Ate logo,*" he said.

Back in the room, I fell asleep until Gini came clattering back in and shook me gently.

"Wake up, Pat," she said. "We're on in thirty-five minutes."

"What are we wearing?" I asked.

"The red and white striped pants and tops and the red shoes."

"I love wearing red and white," I said. "I always feel more zing when I wear it."

"Well, zing yourself into the shower and hurry up."

I sat up, stretched, and went into our luxurious bathroom to get ready.

In thirty minutes flat we were both red and

white striped from head to toe. I felt as if I could dance all night. I started toward the door, but Gini held me back.

"Listen, kiddo," she said. "You know those favela places aren't the safest in the world, don't you?"

"So I've heard," I said. "But I'll be with Yasmin, and she has friends there. I'll be safe as long as I'm with her. Don't worry."

"Well, if you're not back by morning, I'm sending the police after you," she said. We both thought she was kidding.

Pat's Tip for Traveling with Friends: If she's a person who loves nature and you love museums, you might want to take that trip with someone else.

Chapter Twelve

May I Have This Dance?

When we appeared on the dance floor, all the guests stood up and applauded. They kept standing when we started to carioca, moving in place, obviously eager to be up there on the floor with us. When we were really into the swing of the music, moving and twirling, we moved out into the audience and chose men to dance with. My guy was American. He was a little overweight, especially around the middle, and his shirt kept coming out of his pants. He wasn't that great a dancer, but his heart was in the right place and he had a nice smile, so I guided him into the carioca rhythm and led him instead of his leading me.

"This sure is a great place," he said. "I've never been part of a show before."

"Where are you from?" I asked.

"New Jersey," he said. "Ever been there?"

I laughed. "Occasionally," I said. "I'm from Champlain."

"No kidding?" he said. "I'm from Summit. Probably seen you at King's." He was referring to our local supermarket.

"I'm sure of it," I said. "How do you like Rio?"

"I liked it until somebody stole my wallet last night. I'm not so crazy about it now. Caused me a lot of trouble. My wife wants to go home now. She's scared, and I can understand why, but I persuaded her to stay a little longer. Is there anything we should see that we haven't? We've been to Corcovado and Sugar Loaf."

I told him about the flea market. "She can find anything she wants there," I said. "Designer stuff at great prices. I don't even like to shop but I found a great scarf."

"She'll love that. Thanks for telling me about it."

I danced him back to his table and his waiting wife, and he danced with her. When I looked back, I saw her smiling and nodding. I assumed she would get to see the flea market the next day.

We got our usual cheers and applause and bowed to our audience. They kept on dancing after our show was over.

It wasn't eleven yet, so I sneaked across the lobby into Miguel's office to check on my kittens. When I opened the door, one little kitten had jumped out of the basket and was running around the office. I knelt down and he came to me right away. He was my favorite. He had a white collar. He looked up at me. I must have met with his approval because first he gave a little mew and then he purred.

I glanced over at the basket. I could see that Teodora was a little worried about her missing kitten so I brought my cat back to her and put him in the basket next to his mother. Teodora settled back, content, and I patted her too. The kittens were so sweet and cuddly, I wanted to stay there all night, but I knew I had to get ready to meet Yasmin.

They say the world is divided into dog lovers and cat lovers. I know plenty of people who have both dogs and cats, but I am definitely a cat lover. Maybe because I'm basically lazy and don't want to have to walk a dog every day even when it's snowing or raining or freezing cold. A cat just jumps in his litter box and takes care of the whole situation on his own.

There's also something I like about a cat's attitude toward life. They're not as needy as dogs. If you like a cat and want him around, he'll humor you and cuddle up to you and purr as long as you feed him and provide a litter box. If not, he's out of there. A dog will hang around looking for a pat no matter how you treat him.

Best of all, if you want to go away for a week

or two, you just call up a friend and ask her to put food in your cat's dish and water in the other dish and put fresh sand in the litter box. I usually call a friend who also has a cat so I can do the same for her. With dogs, you have to take them to a kennel so someone can walk them every day and look after them.

And maybe it has something to do with the owner's personality. I'm more like a cat. If you like me, that's fine. If you don't, I can feed myself and go to the bathroom all by myself. Dog lovers are often extroverts who bounce into the world eager for people to love them and pat them. Nothing wrong with that. They're just . . . different.

One last pat, and I went upstairs to change into a black top and pants. The red and white outfit was a little too standoutish for this *baile funk*, I thought. Actually, I had no idea what people in the favelas would be wearing, but black seemed to be the safest bet. At eleven, I went back to the lobby and Yasmin was there waiting for me.

"Let's go," she said, pulling me through the door. "We don't want to miss anything." She turned me around to face her. "You didn't tell anyone where you were going, did you?" she said.

I don't know why, but I lied. "No." I said. "No one. Why do you ask?"

"Your friends might be mad that I didn't invite all of you to come. But you understand, Pat, they're very particular about who they let into these things from the outside. They're always afraid the police will get in there and start shooting people."

"The police just shoot people for going to a party?"

"The police shoot people for no reason at all up there," she said. "Nobody cares what happens to poor people. Over 2,000 people a year are killed by the police in these favelas."

She was walking quickly toward the road beside the hotel.

"Aren't we driving up there?" I asked.

"No, it's easier to walk. It's not far."

It seemed far to me and steep. The farther up we walked, the rougher the road became. I was glad I had worn low-heeled shoes.

The closer we got to the top of the hill, the louder the music coming from the favelas blared. It was a combination of African jazz and booty bass from the nineties. It made me want to dance right there on that rutty road.

When we got to the top, the entrance to the favelas was blocked by a huge, old wreck of a car.

"They've closed the whole thing off," Jasmin said. "So the police can't get in."

A large black man appeared on the other side of the car.

"*Quemé?*" he said. Yasmin told me out of the side of her mouth that he was asking, "Who is it?"

"It's me, Yasmin," she said in Portuguese.

There was a rapid exchange of words, which I could not understand, but I assumed she told him that I was a friend of hers and it was safe to let me in. The man motioned for us to climb through the car and follow him.

Since Natalia had not taken us on a tour

through the favelas, I was not prepared for what I saw. *Slums* didn't begin to describe the buildings in front of me. They were worse than shacks, all crowded together, one against the other, no glass in the windows, sewage running in the gutters, walls falling down. It was unbelievable to think of people living there.

Yasmin saw my face. "How'd you like to live like that?" she asked, her voice hard.

"Why don't they do something about it?" I asked.

"Who?" she said, her tone sarcastic.

"The government. Somebody."

"If the government had its way, they would tear all these buildings down and get rid of the people living here. They only put up with them because of the thriving drug trade that goes on here and the people with guns who keep them out."

I didn't say anything. I didn't know what to say. My face must have registered my dismay.

"Cheer up, my little American," Yasmin said. "Let's party."

We rounded the corner and there was a huge open area full of hundreds of people dancing, drinking, yelling, singing. They were all various shades of tan and brown and black. I don't think I was ever as aware of the whiteness of my skin as I was at that moment. The color of my skin was a definite disadvantage. *Hmm, that's a switch,* I thought.

"Are you sure it's all right for us to be here?" I

asked Yasmin. I really meant was it all right for me to be there. Her skin was brown.

"As long as you're with me, you're fine," she said. "I have a lot of friends here."

"How come?" I asked. It didn't seem like her kind of environment.

"I grew up here," she said. "In one of these shacks. My mother had a brief affair with an American. Let's call it a one-nighter. She never saw him again. Nine months later I was born."

It occurred to me she might not be overly fond of Americans. I felt a little uneasy. Let's say, a lot uneasy.

"I thought you said you were from São Paulo," I said.

"I tell people that because I got my education there. I don't want anyone to know about my childhood in the favelas of Rio. I left this hellhole as soon as I could to go to São Paulo and take accounting courses. I came back here and got a job at the Copacabana because my mother was still here in these slums. As soon as I could, I got her out of them and into an apartment near me. But I still feel responsible for the other people I grew up with here. I'd do anything for them. I won't let anything or anyone —"Here she paused and I could see tears in her eyes.

"Yasmin?" I said.

She brushed away the tears and smiled at me. "Come on. Let's dance. Just jump in and move like the great dancer you are. I'll find you later." She gave me a little push, and I found myself next to a bunch of women dancing wildly, crazily, pulling me into the middle of their group.

The music got to me. I didn't care anymore. I put Yasmin out of my mind. I let go of all my inhibitions and careful behavior and nagging anxieties and just danced. I didn't notice people around me. I just gave in to the music. It was like being on some kind of strong drug where my mind stopped working and my body took over. I often wonder where this side of my being came from. It's so spontaneous, compared to the careful, tidy person I am in real life. I cherish this other side of me and am so glad I found my dancing friends who take me all over the world with them.

I don't know how long I danced like that, but after a while I realized I was no longer in a group of women but surrounded by several men moving closer and closer to me. They were all laughing and reaching for me. I looked around for Yasmin, but she was nowhere in sight.

"As long as you're with me, you're fine," she had said. Uh-oh. This was not good. I tried to duck out of the circle of men all around me, but they closed in even more. One of them said something in Portuguese and laughed. He reached for the strap on my top and ripped it off. I lowered my head and smashed it into his groin as hard as I could. He yelled and dropped back just long enough for me to slip through his legs and get away.

Luckily, it was dark, and I was in black. I scooted in and out of other dancing groups, getting farther and farther away from the men who had closed in on me. Most people were too caught up in the dance and drugs and drinking to pay much attention to me. I kept trying to spot Yasmin in that crowd, but I couldn't find her anywhere. Finally I got back to the car that was blocking the street, climbed over the top of it, and ran down the hill to the hotel.

I stumbled through the doorway. There was no one in the lobby. It must have been about two in the morning. I got in the elevator and leaned against the wall until I reached my floor.

When I opened our door, Gini was sitting up fast asleep. I turned off the light and tried to be quiet, but I was still so scared, I groaned as I fell onto the bed. Gini opened her eyes, turned on the light, took one look at me, and was instantly awake.

"Pat!" she said. "What happened to you? You look terrible."

I realized my top was nearly torn off, my hair was in my eyes, and my face must have been a mess.

I started to cry. I couldn't stop. I tried to blurt out what had happened to me, but the words wouldn't come. "I . . . I was . . . Oh, Gini, it was . . ."

In a flash she was out of her bed and sitting on mine. She put her arms around me and rocked me. "Shh, Pat, it's all right. Hush, hush, you're safe."

Gradually my sobs subsided, and I mopped my eyes and blew my nose.

When I could talk, the whole story of my experience at the *baile funk* poured out. The music. The dancing. The men. The torn strap. The terror.

"My God!" Gini said. "Where was Yasmin while you were going through all of this?"

"I think she meant to disappear and leave me there," I said. "Gini, you should have seen the way she looked at me when she was telling me about her childhood, about her American father who got her mother pregnant and left, about growing up in those slums. You wouldn't believe the way people live in those favelas. Worse than any slums I've ever seen, anywhere. I think she hates Americans because of her deadbeat father. She must have wanted something really bad to happen to me tonight. Because I'm an American, I mean."

"How strange," Gini said. "She's usually so low-key and unemotional. Are you going to tell the police?"

"What am I going to tell them—that I went to a street dance in the favelas, and some guy I don't know ripped the strap off my top, and I couldn't find Yasmin. They're going to ask me why I went there in the first place. They'll blame it on me for being so stupid."

"Well, it won't hurt to tell Chief Pereira tomorrow," Gini said. "I can't get rid of this feeling that Yasmin is somehow mixed up in these murders. I don't know what it is, but it has something to do with money and her job here and your experience with her tonight and—you know what I mean?"

"We have no proof of that, Gini. None at all. She may have finked out on me tonight because I'm American, but that doesn't connect her to the murders. Even I don't believe that, and I'm ready to believe anything bad about her."

"I know that, but it would be interesting to find out why she really disappeared while you were being molested by her friends. I can't believe it's just because you're an American. That's why you should tell Pereira what happened."

"That still doesn't mean she had anything to do with the murders. She just doesn't like me."

"How could anybody not like you?" Gini said. "Miss Lovable."

"Right," I said. "Sorry I woke you, Gini. Go back to sleep."

"I'm so sorry I fell asleep waiting for you, Pat. Are you sure you're OK?"

"More or less," I said. "I can still feel their hands on my shoulder."

"Try to sleep," she said.

I stripped off my torn clothes and was asleep in seconds.

Pat's Tip for Traveling with Friends: If you're no good at details like best plane fares, least expensive hotels, and travel discounts, go with someone who is.

Chapter Thirteen

What's Shrimp Bobo?

The next morning I couldn't make myself get out of bed. I kept turning over and burying my head under the pillow and going back to sleep. Every time I woke up, I remembered the night before and the circle of men closing in on me. I heard that loud music. Saw the broken-down buildings, the sewage running down the streets. I could not get out of bed and face the world.

About ten o'clock, the door to our suite opened, and Gini poked her head inside. When she saw me still buried under the covers, she came over to the bed and sat down beside me.

"Are you OK, Pat?" she asked.

"Not really," I mumbled, peeking around the sheet.

She gave me a hug. "It's over, hon," she said. "You're safe. Natalia is taking us up to Grumari for lunch on the Barra da Tijuca Beach, and then she said she would take us to a museum of Brazilian folk art that we would love. Do you want to come with us or do you want to just rest today? I told our gang what happened to you last night, and they're all worried about you."

I sat up and rubbed my eyes. "I really want to come with you. I don't want to stay here by myself. I need to get away from this hotel. Could you ask them to wait while I get dressed?"

"Sure, don't worry," Gini said. "Natalia said to take as long as you need. She'll wait for you."

She hesitated and then said, "The strangest thing, Pat. Yasmin stopped by our table this morning while we were eating breakfast and asked where you were. She said she looked everywhere for you last night but couldn't find you. She wanted to know if you were all right."

"What?" I yelled. "She had the nerve to say she—I don't believe her!" I was sputtering, barely able to get the words out.

"I couldn't believe it either, Pat. I stared at her and then I said—you know me, I can't help it—I said, 'Where were *you* last night? Pat came home a wreck after being attacked and said you weren't anywhere around.' "

"What did she say to that?" I asked.

"She said, her voice quivering, 'Oh, I'm so sorry! How terrible. I looked all over for her but when I didn't see her I just assumed she went back to the hotel. I had no idea she . . .' "

I shivered. "She meant to leave me there last night," I said. "What a liar. Just keep her away from me, will you? I don't want to have anything more to do with her."

"I'll try, but you're going to have to confront her sooner or later," Gini said. I knew she was right. Just not this morning.

"I'll order you a couple of rolls and some coffee," Gini said. "Whenever you're ready, come on downstairs and we'll head to Grumari."

She left. I stumbled out of bed and shuddered when I saw my favorite black top and pants lying on the floor crumpled and torn. I went into the luxurious bathroom and turned on the blessedly hot water in the shower. I scrubbed every part of me several times. I felt like I was washing away the night before.

When I felt clean enough, I toweled off and put on a crisp white shirt and black jeans. I brushed my hair dry, put on some makeup, and went downstairs to join the others. I felt tense. I was so afraid I would run into Yasmin. I had no idea what I would say to her. I was out of luck. She was there in the lobby.

"Pat!" she said, coming over to me and putting her arms around me. I froze, then pulled away from her. "Whatever happened to you last night? I looked everywhere for you. I was really worried about you."

I looked at her in disbelief. At first I couldn't even answer her. Then I said, "Maybe you should

have looked a little harder, Yasmin. I was lucky
to get out of there alive. You should have made
sure I was all right. I looked everywhere for you
when those men were after me and you weren't
there. Didn't you wonder if I was all right?" I was
trying to talk in a normal tone of voice, but my
voice got louder as that terrifying night came
back to me in a rush.

"I was there all along," she said. *Liar,* I thought.
"But it was very dark so I'm not surprised you
couldn't find me. I did look for you, Pat, but in
that crowd it was hard to find anybody. Everybody was moving around, dancing, the music
was loud. I was sure you had enough and went
back to the Copacabana without me."

"I guess I was too busy getting away from that
bunch of men who were trying to tear my
clothes off," I said and walked away from her.

She didn't follow me. She stood there in the
lobby and watched me join my friends in the
dining room.

"Oh, hi, Pat," Gini said. "Here are the rolls
and coffee I promised you. I was just about to
bring them upstairs to you."

"Thanks, Gini," I said and buttered a warm
roll to eat with the hot, delicious coffee she put
in front of me.

"Are you all right, my little Hoofer?" Natalia
said, a worried look on her face. "Gini was telling
us about your experience last night. Don't you
know you should never go near those favelas
without some protection?"

"I thought I had protection," I said, looking

toward the lobby, but Yasmin was no longer there. "Yasmin assured me that as long as I was with her, I'd be fine. The only trouble was she disappeared, and I definitely wasn't fine."

Natalia's face closed down. She didn't say anything. Just looked at me. Not in a compassionate way. It was impossible to tell what she was thinking.

"Next time take us with you," Tina said.

"You're usually so careful," Mary Louise said. "What made you decide to do that?"

"I thought I'd be carefree and spontaneous for once," I said. "Thought that I was completely safe with Yasmin. You know she told me she grew up in that favela." I told them the story of her mother and the American rotter who got her pregnant with Yasmin and then deserted her. About Yasmin going to São Paulo to learn to be an accountant and then coming back here to rescue her mother from the favelas.

"Don't go anywhere else with her alone," Gini said. "You shouldn't trust her."

"You think?" I said, finishing up my coffee. "I wouldn't go to the shop next door with her." I needed to change the subject. "So, Natalia, where are we going today?" I asked her.

The sparkle popped back on that pretty face. Amazing how she could just turn it on and off. "I want to take you up the coast for lunch in a wonderful restaurant in Grumari, overlooking the beach." she said. "It has a gorgeous view and the best shrimp in the city. Then, on the way back, you have to see this Casa do Pontal museum of Brazilian folk art. Hundreds and hundreds of little figures of people, working, eating, sleeping, making babies—wait till you see. It's a trip."

It sounded like something I really needed to restore my sanity. "Let's go!" I said.

Our faithful Ramon was outside waiting for us. Natalia ushered us into the van, avoiding my eyes, bustling about, and then settling into the front seat.

"Are you ladies comfortable back there?" Ramon asked, as he started the engine.

"We're fine, Ramon. Thank you," Tina said.

"Just let me know if you need anything," he said, looking over his shoulder and smiling at us. I was grateful that he was our driver. He seemed to care about us.

It seemed to take forever to get to Grumari. Ramon had said it was only about an hour and half away, but the roads were so crowded and narrow in places it actually took much longer. We didn't talk much. Even Natalia was uncharacteristically quiet. We passed streamlined white office buildings, tall apartment buildings, cafés, shops, all crowded together in this busy city. After about an hour, we came to the small town of Grumari.

"We're almost there, guys," Natalia said. "The restaurant is at the top of a mountain."

We left the streets of the town and followed a narrow, winding road up the mountain through a forest of thick trees and greenery until we arrived at Point de Grumari.

"All the food is good here," Natalia said. "Es-

pecially their seafood. But people come here
for their giant shrimp. You can get it cooked in
lots of different ways, but get the shrimp bobo.
And you have to drink Chopp—that's beer—
with it."

"What if we don't like beer?" Mary Louise
said.

"Drink it anyway," Natalia said. "Come on,
Mary Louise, it's traditional. Anyway, it's really
good beer. Not like the kind you get at home."
Then she realized she had a nondrinker present
spoiling all the fun.

"And for you, Pat," she said, "they have a
spectacular lemon squash. Or papaya juice."

Just what I yearned for—lemon squash or papaya juice. Not.

Natalia led us into the restaurant where she
was greeted effusively by the owner and his wife.
They kissed her on both cheeks and the owner
said, "Indoors or out, Natalia?"

"You know I'm an outdoor girl," she said.

She introduced us to Senhor and Senhora
Santos, who took us through the sunlit dining
room, with large uncurtained windows that made
the whole restaurant shine with the beauty of an
oceanside view. But that view paled beside the
scene that awaited us in the outdoor patio, overlooking the Marambaia Sandbank. Stretching
for twenty-six miles, the white sand made a long
ribbon of white along the water's edge.

"That's the Sepetiba Lagoon down there,"
Natalia said. "The marshes around it are on the
Marambaia Sandbank. Up to our right is the

national park. There's probably no more beautiful view anywhere. But even better than the view is their shrimp. Wait till you taste their shrimp!"

"I know, Natalia," Senhora Santos said. "You don't have to tell me. Shrimp bobo and beer all around—yes?"

Natalia checked with us. We all agreed. We'd come for the shrimp. And I, of course, came for the shrimp and lemon squash. What can I tell you? You can get used to anything!

I breathed in the fresh sea air, leaned back in my chair, and enjoyed this respite from murder and *baile funk*s. I didn't want to think about anything except this lovely place and being with my best friends in the world.

"How did you gorgeous girls end up dancing in a hotel in Rio de Janeiro?" Natalia asked. Oh, good. A nice safe subject.

"Somebody saw us dance on a train in northern Spain and told Senhor Ortega about us," Tina said. "He saw our YouTube video and hired us."

"Do you actually earn a living dancing?" she asked.

"Not really," Tina said. "We all have other jobs—except Mary Louise. She works at home. But it's more fun than anything else we've ever done. We're hooked."

"What do you do besides dancing with strange men at the Copacabana?" Natalia asked.

Tina laughed. "Well, I'm the travel editor at a bridal magazine, Gini is a documentary filmmaker, Janice is an actress and director on Broadway, Pat is a family therapist, and Mary Louise is a housewife."

"Sounds thoroughly respectable," Natalia said. "Did you just decide to run away and dance one day?"

"We went to a dance class because it was good exercise," Mary Louise said. "And we fell in love with dancing. We worked out a whole routine."

"Then we did this YouTube video for the fun of it," Gini said. "Some guy in Russia saw it and hired us to dance on a cruise ship. Then we just kept getting hired—on a train in northern Spain, on a bateau mouche in Paris, and now in Rio. I don't know how it happened, but I hope it never stops."

"Were you always a singer, Natalia?" Janice asked.

Natalia looked out at the lagoon for a moment, a serious look on her face.

"Actually, I started out as a dancer too," she said. "I love dancing. But I kept getting hired as a singer, so that's what I am."

"How did you learn to speak English so well?" Tina asked.

"My mother was an American who married a Brazilian here in Rio," she said. "She taught me English before she deserted me and my two little sisters and went back to California when I was eight years old. We never saw her again."

There was silence around the table. Americans weren't coming off so well in this Rio experience. First Yasmin, whose American father was a rat, and now Natalia's mother, who wasn't all that great either. Tina broke the silence.

"I have a great idea," Tina said. "On our last night here, why don't you dance with us?"

"I'd love that!" Natalia said. "I need to rehearse with you though. Will we have time for that?"

"We can do that when we get back this afternoon," Tina said.

"If nobody else gets killed," Gini said.

"Bite your tongue, Gini," I said. "We've had enough murders. And nobody seems to have the slightest idea who is doing it. Or, I guess I should say, there seems to be too many people who might have a reason for doing it. But none of it makes any sense."

Natalia started to say something and then stopped.

"Natalia?" Gini said. "Still think it's Lucas murdering people right and left?"

"Who else is there?" she said. "Miguel hasn't got the guts. Yasmin had no reason to kill any of them. It has to be Lucas."

"What about you?" I asked before I could stop myself. Why did I say that? My friends looked at me as if I had lost my mind.

"Pat," Tina said, "that's a strange . . ."

"Oh, forgive me, Natalia," I said. "I don't know what made me say that. Of course I don't think you could kill anybody. I'm sorry."

Natalia patted my arm. "It's OK, Pat," she said.

"I know you didn't mean it. You're still upset after last night. I don't blame you."

"You're right," I said. "I am still upset. Makes me say things I don't mean."

"I understand," Natalia said.

Senhor Santos appeared with our shrimp bobo, five icy cold mugs of beer, and one lemon squash. By the time he finished serving us the shrimp, rice, and a salad, my rude question was forgotten in the enjoyment of our fantastic lunch.

It was divine. These huge shrimp basking in some kind of fantastic stewlike sauce tasted like no other shrimp I'd ever had.

"Natalia, could you please get the recipe for this," Mary Louise said. "I have to make this for George. He loves shrimp."

"Of course, my little chef," Natalia said. "I will see that you get it."

We finished our shrimp without the subject of murder coming up again and were sipping our coffee contentedly.

"Finish up, ladies," Natalia said. "I want to take you to the folk museum next, and then we have to get back to the hotel so I can practice with you. I'm so looking forward to this."

Reluctantly we drank up our lovely strong coffee and got up to leave. We thanked Senhor Santos and his wife, who gave Natalia the recipe for the shrimp bobo, and took off with Ramon for the museum of Brazilian folk art.

Shrimp Bobo

3 lbs. very large shrimp, peeled and deveined
3 lbs. cassava
2 cups chopped onions
3 cloves garlic, chopped
½ cup olive oil
1 35 oz. can whole tomatoes
¼ cup chopped cilantro
2 cups coconut milk
¼ cup palm oil
Salt and pepper to taste

1. Cook the peeled cassava until it's tender. About fifteen minutes.
2. Drain the cassava and save the water it cooked in.
3. Mash the cassava with a fork. Set aside.
4. Sauté the onion and garlic in olive oil.
5. Stir half of the cilantro and tomatoes into the cooked onion and garlic.
6. Add the shrimp to the mixture and cook about fifteen minutes.
7. Stir in the mashed cassava.
8. Add some of the water the cassava cooked in if the mixture is too dry.
9. Add coconut milk, the rest of the cilantro, and the palm oil.
10. Season with salt and pepper.
11. Serve with cold beer.

Pat's Tip for Traveling with Friends: If she's a morning person and you're a night owl, take that into account when you're planning your days.

Chapter Fourteen

What Are Those People Doing?

"I think you'll really like this museum," Natalia said. "It's not like any other I've ever seen."

"What's so different about it?" Gini asked.

"Well, it has every kind of art mixed together," Natalia said. "Some paintings and sculpture, but mostly little figures representing every aspect of life. And there's one room I won't tell you about. I want you to discover it on your own." She giggled. "You'll find it very interesting."

Ramon pulled up in front of the museum. It looked small on the outside. It was a two-story building with one bright red wall on a white structure with lots of windows. When we went inside, I understood what Natalia was trying to tell us. There were thousands of small clay figures in glass cases, other animated figurines spread out on separate tables, a life-size figure winding a music box, and all sorts of other exhibits I couldn't wait to see. Natalia was right. I had never been in a museum like this before.

We each wandered off on our own, as we usually do. I found a display of little plastic figures in a miniature circus. They were all moving. A cute little woman slid down a rope. A man rode a bicycle on a rod suspended in air. A trapeze artist swung from a bar. An audience seated on the side applauded. Each tiny person was different from all the others.

Jan beckoned to me from a separate, closed-off room. "Pat, come look at this. You won't believe it."

I followed her into the room. At first I thought it was just more tiny Brazilians working, playing, going to the dentist, lying on a stretcher in the hospital, going about their ordinary lives in ordinary ways. Then I took a closer look and couldn't believe my eyes. These small perverts were performing every kind of sex act you could imagine and some I could never have imagined in my wildest dreams. Jan was laughing as she watched me react to this pornographic display.

"Whose idea was this?" I asked. "I've never seen anything like this before in a museum—or anywhere else, for that matter."

"Somebody with a very active sex life, I guess,"

Jan said, not able to stop laughing. "Let's find Mary Louise."

We both thought it was a hilarious idea to show this naughty exhibit to our innocent Hoofer. We peeked out the door and saw Mary Louise checking out the guitar-playing manikin nearby. She hadn't noticed our wicked room yet.

"Psst, Weezie," Jan said. "Come see this. It's not like anything else in the museum."

She walked over to us. "This is the weirdest museum I've ever been in," she said. "What have you found?"

"Come in here and see for yourself," Janice said.

"OK," she said. "Why do you have that funny look on your face, Jan?" She started to go in the room but stopped.

"Why does it say NO CHILDREN ALLOWED on the door?" she asked. "What's in there, you guys?"

"You'll see," I said, grabbing her arm and pulling her inside.

Jan and I watched her as she looked at the glass shelves full of sex-crazed human beings.

"Who did this?" she said, shocked and angry at first until she saw us laughing in the corner. "You two are disgusting."

"We didn't do it," Jan said. "But we knew you'd love it. Some of the people look just like you and George."

"I'm never speaking to either one of you again!" Mary Louise said, laughing in spite of herself. "I'm leaving to look at some more wholesome Brazilians."

She walked out of the porn room and bumped into Natalia.

"Ah, I see you've found the most educational of all the exhibits here," Natalia said when we came out of the room. "How'd you like it?"

"Wild," Janice said. "Nothing like that in the Met at home."

"Some things you have to come to Brazil for," Natalia said. "We'd better round up the others and head back to the hotel. It's getting late, and it will take us at least an hour to get back to the Copacabana."

"We can't leave before Gini and Tina see this room," Janice said. She found our friends around the corner enjoying the circus exhibit and whisked them into the naughty room before they knew what was happening to them.

One whoop of joy from Gini and I knew we were right in not leaving before she saw the many bodily entanglements presented there. Tina came out trying to look at least a little disapproving, but she didn't succeed.

"If you Hoofers have had your fun for the day," Natalia said, enjoying Gini's reaction, "we'd better get back to more mundane things like our rehearsal for tonight back at the hotel."

Not at all chastened, Gini followed us into the van. "Wish I could have photographed those little devils," she said.

We chattered all the way home about our scrumptious lunch in Grumari, about the folksy art in the museum, and about our exciting four days in Rio. We only had one more day in the city, and we couldn't decide whether we were happy or sad to be leaving.

"I feel like we're leaving before the movie is over," Gini said. "Three people are dead and we're going home before we found out who killed them. It doesn't seem right."

"I'd just as soon leave before anyone else is killed—like one of us," I said.

"That chief of police seems very intelligent," Tina said. "Maybe he'll find the killer before we leave."

"Then he should ask Yasmin some more questions," I said. "She's hiding something. I know she is. I think she knows who the killer is. She might even be the killer herself."

Natalia turned away from us and looked out the front of the van.

"Why do you say that, Pat?" Mary Louise said. "What makes you think she's guilty?"

"She had some reason to leave me in a really dangerous situation the other night at that street party," I said. "She thinks I know more than I do, and she wanted something bad to happen to me."

"You don't know that, Pat," Tina said. "She probably didn't mean to leave you there. It was a big crowd and it was dark."

"She meant it, Tina," I said. "If you'd been there with someone trying to tear your clothes off, you'd know she wasn't watching over you."

"Pat's right," Gini said. Good old Gini. "Yasmin thinks Pat knows more than she really does."

Natalia turned around to face us again. Her

face was deadly serious. I had only seen her look like that a couple of times since she started guiding us around. And come to think of it, it was usually when someone mentioned Yasmin. What was that all about?

"I'm sure you're wrong, Gini," she said. "Yasmin would never do anything like that. If you want to know the ending to your movie, you should concentrate on Lucas. He's the guilty one."

Gini pinched my arm. I got her message. *Don't say any more about this now.* I knew she was right and changed the subject.

"Where are you taking us tomorrow on our last day, Natalia?"

"I haven't decided yet," she said. "Let me think about it."

Ramon pulled up in front of the hotel, and we jumped out.

"Meet you in the Piano Bar in half an hour," Natalia said. "We'll dance."

Pat's Tip for Traveling with Friends: Travel with someone who loves to take care of all the details like plane times, location of the hotel, best restaurants, all available discounts. Relax, and let her do it.

Chapter Fifteen

Not Again!

We separated to change into our rehearsal clothes. I wanted to see my kittens again, so I went down to the lobby while Gini was still dressing.

There was no one in Miguel's office. I knelt down beside Teodora, who was taking a nap. Only one little kitten was in the basket with her. The others were running all around the office, exploring, playing, tumbling about, having fun. The kitten with the white collar whom I loved the most came up to me and crawled into my lap. He knew me! I picked him up and patted him and he licked my hand.

"I wish I could take you home with me," I said to him. "You'd love my Eliza."

"You're quite the cat lover, aren't you?" a harsh voice said. Yasmin was standing in front of me, pointing a gun at me. "I like dogs myself."

I put the kitten in the basket with his mother, and scrambled to my feet.

"Yasmin! What are you doing with that gun?"

"I heard what you've been saying about me," she said, "that you think I might be the murderer. I don't need anyone saying things like that. You've been telling people bad things about me since we went to the *baile funk*. I don't know what you think you know about me, but I'm going to get rid of you before you blab to the police. It's time you got lost in the favelas and don't find your way out again."

"Are you crazy?" I said. "You can't get away with this. My friends are waiting for me to rehearse with them. If I don't show up, they'll have the police out looking for me before you can get me up the hill."

"We're not walking this time," she said. "My friend will drive us up there. He's waiting outside right now. We'll be there in a few minutes before your friends even notice you're gone. You'll disappear as soon as we get there. One injection of my never-fail drug, and you'll be comparing notes with Maria, Sumiko, and Gabriel before you know it."

"I don't know anything, Yasmin," I said, stalling for time. "I have no reason to think you killed anybody."

"That's not what you said in the car coming back from Grumari today," she said.

Natalia. Natalia must have told her what I said. I couldn't believe it. Funny, friendly, kind Natalia.

"Is Natalia in this with you?" I asked.

"Who said anything about Natalia?" she said. "Not me."

"But why did you kill them?"

"Who said I killed anybody?" she said. "You're the one who thinks I'm a murderer. Now shut up and go through the other door of this office to the alley in the back of the hotel. My friend is waiting for us there."

She pointed the gun at me and gestured toward the door.

"One sound out of you and I kill your cat friend over there," she said.

The thought of my five little kittens without a mother kept me from screaming. Also the gun against my back. I walked to the door and saw Ramon waiting in one of the hotel's cars, the same one we had taken on our sight-seeing trips with Natalia. Ramon. Sweet, helpful, gentle Ramon. He was Yasmin's friend.

He smiled as I got into the car. "*Bom dia,* senhora," he said.

I didn't answer. I still couldn't believe it. He must have been the one who told Yasmin what I said in the car this afternoon, not Natalia. That was a relief. I didn't want to think Natalia was in on this.

When we were in the car, I said to Yasmin, "You can at least tell me why you killed those three people. And don't tell me you didn't. You owe me that if you're going to kill me."

"I don't owe you anything, you silly American Hoofer," she said, her voice hard with the hatred she felt for my country.

"What harm would it do for you to tell me?" I said. "I'll be dead. I can't tell anyone."

She pushed the gun against my side harder. "I guess it doesn't matter anymore what you know," she said. She looked out the window. "Drive into the favelas, Ramon. You know the house I want."

He nodded.

"My mother is very ill." She stopped. When she continued, her words caught in her throat. I could tell her emotion was making it difficult for her to talk. "I needed a lot of money to take care of her. I wanted to be sure she had the best doctors. I didn't make enough at the hotel, and they don't provide medical insurance. They're cheap. So I provided my own insurance. I took a certain percentage of the money the hotel got each week for myself. They owed that to me. I was in charge of the records, so it was easy to hide what I took." She stopped. "What's the matter, Ramon? Why did you stop?"

"There's a cart turned over in the road and the street is too narrow to go around it. I have to move it."

"Well, hurry up. I want to get this over with."

"Right away, senhora," Ramon said, and got out of the car.

"But why did you kill Maria? Did she find out what you were doing?" I asked.

"Yeah. That little rat nosed around and found out. She was blackmailing me. She didn't get enough from Lucas or the hotel to pay for all her expensive clothes, so she held me up for some money every month. She kept raising the amount until finally I had to get rid of her. People were beginning to ask questions."

"Did Dr. Souza give you the anesthetic you used to kill her?" I asked.

"No, no. I took it from his supply. He wasn't very careful about locking it up. He had a lot of it stashed in his room because he used it when he operated in the local hospital. I could get a key to any of the rooms I wanted. I waited until he was busy somewhere else and helped myself to whatever I needed. He didn't miss it at first because he had so much."

"Then why did you kill him?

"Because eventually, after the medical examiner figured out that both Maria and Sumiko died of this drug, the police assumed he did it. He told them someone else had stolen the anesthetic. He knew I had a key to his room and he confronted me. I denied it and said anybody could have had a key made. Unfortunately, one time after a drink or two, I had told him about Maria blackmailing me. I don't know why I did that. I should swear off drinking—like you. Anyway, he said he was going to tell the police about that, so I had to kill him."

"And Sumiko?" I asked. "Why did you kill her?"

Ramon got back in the car and we continued our ascent up the hill.

"She got nosy too. She spent money like water, and she knew we were taking in more money than showed up in the records. She was a smart little cookie and had studied accounting herself before she married her meal ticket, Miguel. She went through the books one time when I was in the hospital with my mother. She started asking too many questions and threatened to tell Miguel that she knew what I was doing. I had to get rid of her, too, because she knew too much."

"What makes you think I knew any of this?" I asked.

"I didn't know how much you knew, but when I heard what you said in the car, that you suspected me, I knew I had to get rid of you too. You don't understand. I would do anything I have to do to take care of my mother."

"But they'll know you did it," I said. "They'll find me here and know it was you who killed me."

"You don't think I'm going to stick around here, do you?" she said. "I've stashed away enough for my mother's medical and living expenses for both of us to last me for the rest of my life. I'll take her to São Paulo, where she'll be safe. I owe her everything."

"Where is your mother now?" I asked.

"She's waiting for us in the hole I grew up in. She doesn't live there anymore, but I told her to meet us there. She doesn't like Americans any more than I do, so she's glad to help me get rid of you. I need Ramon to stay in the car in case we need to get away in a hurry. My mother will hold the gun on you while I inject you with this lovely little going-away drug."

Ramon drove more slowly through the crowded streets of the favelas, getting deeper into the filth and poverty on all sides. Children were splashing in the dirty water. Men passed out on drugs were slumped against the walls of the hovels. I couldn't believe people could survive in this place. It looked like I wasn't going to either.

Ramon stopped at the end of an alley. Yasmin pushed me out of the car and shoved me through a doorway into a tiny room with no furniture. A small woman, her face ravaged by illness, greeted Yasmin as she came in.

"You are sure you want to kill this American?" she asked in a low voice.

"Yes, *mãe*," she said. "She talks too much. We have to move quickly. Our bags are in the car. Ramon will drive us to São Paulo once we get rid of her."

"If you're sure," she said. "Give me the gun. Hurry up."

Yasmin knocked me to the ground and gave the gun to her mother.

"Don't move," she said to me. "My mother knows how to use that gun very well. She had to learn that living in this place."

She opened her bag and took out a bottle of the anesthetic and a syringe.

There had to be a way out of this. I couldn't die like this. *Please, God*, I prayed. *Help me find a way out of this.*

Suddenly, Yasmin's mother's face contorted in intense pain. She bent over, her eyes closed. I leaped at her, grabbed the gun, and pointed it at Yasmin.

"Give me that syringe," I said. She dropped the filled hypodermic needle on the floor. I smashed it with my foot.

"Get your mother in the car," I said. She hesitated.

"Now," I said, putting the gun against her head. "I mean it."

Yasmin's mother was doubled up in pain on the floor. Yasmin had to pick her up and carry her in her arms to the car.

Ramon started to get out of the car to come at me.

"Don't move, Ramon, or I'll shoot," I said. "I'm used to guns." I'd never held one in my life before, but he didn't know that. "You're going to take us back to police headquarters."

Yasmin sat down in the backseat holding her mother. Ramon started the engine. I opened the side door and had one foot in the car when Ramon hit the accelerator hard. I fell backward into the street and shot at the car, trying to hit one of the tires. But just then a couple of little children ran into the road to see what was happening, and I couldn't fire the gun again.

I went back in the house, picked up the bottle with the anesthetic in it, and put it and the gun in my bag. I had to get out of there. By now several people who had heard the gunshots came out of their shacks to see what was going on. I ducked down and managed to get around the corner and onto the street that led out of the favelas before anyone stopped me. Then I ran. I ran for my life. Through the broken streets. Past the hopeless lives and shattered huts that somehow managed to exist in this rich city.

I could hear shouts in back of me, but I kept going until I got out of the favelas and made it to the Copacabana. I collapsed on the floor of the lobby. The man behind the desk ran to me. "Senhora, senhora," he said. He hurried to the Piano Bar and my friends and Natalia surrounded me.

"Pat! Are you all right? What happened to you?" Tina asked.

I couldn't talk. I was out of breath from running down that hill, away from death, away from the horror.

They lifted me up and carried me into Miguel's office.

"Watch out . . ." I stammered. "The kittens."

There were little cats everywhere, under the desk, on top of the desk, in the basket, under the chairs. Teodora was clearly alarmed. Her meow was a cry of warning to her babies.

My friends put me on the couch in Miguel's office and knelt beside me.

When I could talk, I told them what had happened. I showed them the syringe and gun in my purse.

"My God, Pat," Gini said. "Thank heavens you got away. You could have been . . ."

"Yes, I could have been," I said. "If Yasmin's mother hadn't collapsed like that, I would be lying on the floor up there dead." I started to shake.

"Where is Yasmin now?" Natalia asked.

"On her way to São Paulo, I assume," I said.

Miguel was already on the phone to the police.

"Pereira is coming," he said. "He's sending men after the car. I told him it was one of the hotel's cars and gave him the license plate number."

I felt as if I could never get up from that couch. I was shaking all over. I didn't want to move—ever.

"Tina," I said, "I don't think I can dance tonight."

"You don't have to, hon. Just take it easy."

Mary Louise picked up a kitten near the couch and gave it to me to hold. It was my little white-collared kitten. He mewed and licked my hand. The feel of that furry little angel helped to calm me down.

Tina brought me a cup of coffee. I put my kitten down to take the cup, but my hand was shaking so much, I had to put the cup on the table.

The door of the office opened and Chief Pereira came in.

"Senhora," he said, "are you all right?"

"Not really," I said.

He sat down beside me. "Tell me what happened, if you can."

I told him the whole story about Yasmin abducting me with a gun, about the favela where she took me, about the syringe and the anesthetic, about her mother, about Ramon. It all came out in a rush, and then I couldn't talk anymore.

"We'll get them," he said. "We have the license plate number of the car. They'll be picked up within the hour."

His cell phone rang. He listened and then looked grim.

"They found the car abandoned in a parking lot near the beach. They must be hiding out someplace near here until they can get another car and get to São Paulo."

Near here. That's all I needed to hear to start shaking again.

Pereira took my hand in his. "They won't be anywhere near you, senhora," he said. "Do not worry."

Right. I was beyond worry. I was a basket case.

"I need to go to my room and sleep for a while," I said. "Can you guys help me get there, please?"

Gini and Tina raised me up and got me on my feet.

"We'll talk more when you're feeling better, senhora," the police chief said.

"Thank you," I said, and leaned on my two friends to get to the elevator and my room. They helped me onto the bed, slid off my shoes, and tiptoed out. I was already asleep by the time they closed the door.

Pat's Tip for Traveling with Friends: Don't travel with a smoker.

Chapter Sixteen

Surprise!

I don't know how long I slept, but I was awakened by the door of the suite closing. Someone had come into the room. I opened my eyes. Natalia was standing there next to the bed.

"Natalia," I said, surprised to see her. "What are you doing here? What do you want?"

"Shhhh," she said. "Don't make a sound."

Then I saw that she was holding a gun. No, I thought. No. This can't be happening. Not twice in the same day.

"What are you doing with that gun?" I said. I was too sleepy and confused to make sense out of what was happening.

"What do you think?" she said. The flibbertigibbet, fluttery, laugh-a-minute Natalia was gone.

In her place was a tough-looking woman who meant business. She was dressed in black and wore a black cap covering her flame-colored hair.

"We're getting out of here." she said. "Yasmin and her mother are waiting for us, and we're taking my car to São Paulo. No one will be looking for me. And if they are, we have you as a hostage."

"You're mixed up in these murders?" I said, still too out of it to understand what was happening. This was Natalia. Adorable little Natalia. Harmless Natalia.

"Shut up and get up. I want to get you out of here before anyone comes looking for you."

"Listen, Natalia. I don't have the strength to follow you anywhere. I was almost killed a couple of hours ago. Go ahead and shoot me. I can't move."

"You may not care if I kill you, but how would you like it if I killed that cat and her kittens in Miguel's office?"

"You'd do that?" I asked.

"Watch me," she said. "I hate cats."

The thought of my little kitten dying was too much to bear. I dragged myself out of that bed, put on my shoes, and followed her out of the suite and down some back stairs to her car in the parking lot. It must have been about six o'clock. Nobody saw us. Natalia pushed me into the backseat of the car. Yasmin and her mother were hiding on the floor. Ramon was nowhere in sight. Natalia gave Yasmin her gun.

"Ah, there you are, my American friend," Yasmin said, getting up from the floor and sitting next to me on the seat. "We meet again. This time you won't be so lucky."

She helped her mother, her eyes closed, her face pale, into the seat next to her. I couldn't believe this was happening. I made up my mind that if I got through this alive I would never leave my house again. I'd never go on another dancing tour as long as I lived. I'd just curl up in a little ball and let Denise take care of me until I died of old age.

"Why don't we just shoot her now and get it over with?" Yasmin asked Natalia.

"Because we might need her if we're stopped," Natalia said.

"But it'll take us at least six hours to get to São Paulo," Yasmin said. "We don't want to keep her around all that time."

"When we're about halfway there, we'll throw her out of the car and keep going. Nobody will be looking for us anyway."

That Natalia was all heart.

"Won't those Hoofers wonder where you are at the performance tonight?" Yasmin asked.

"They're not dancing tonight," Natalia said. "This Hoofer begged off. Seems she had some sort of terrible experience in the favelas this afternoon."

They both laughed.

"It's only six now," Natalia continued. "They think she's sleeping and they won't check on her for a while. We've got at least a couple of hours before they find out she's not in her room. You've got our money with you, right?"

"Of course. You'll get your share as soon as we get there."

"You better be sure I do," Natalia said, her voice hard. "What did you do with Ramon? I thought he'd be with you."

"He didn't want to go to São Paulo," Yasmin said. "He went back to the favelas where he can hide out with his druggy friends. The police will never find him."

"OK, let's get out of here," Natalia said. "Don't take your eyes off our American friend. She's a tricky one. Remember, she got away from you once today."

She started the engine and backed the car out of the hotel parking lot. There were other people in the lot getting in or out of their cars, but nobody noticed us. Natalia expertly steered the car onto the crowded street and headed south.

My brain went into emergency mode. How was I going to get out of here before they pushed me out onto the highway? *When in doubt, ask some questions,* I decided. I didn't know what else to do.

"So, Natalia, how are you involved in all this?" I asked her.

She was weaving in and out of the heavy traffic and didn't answer me. "Yasmin," I said, "tell me how Natalia got involved in this whole thing."

She looked first at her mother to be sure she was all right. Her mother's eyes were closed and she seemed to be breathing more easily.

"You don't need to tell her anything," Natalia said, passing cars on the right.

I don't know why—maybe she was bored—but Yasmin decided to talk to me.

"Well, if you must know, she wanted to get out of Rio and go to New York to get a job singing there, but she needed money to get there. She knew I must be doing some fancy accounting. Natalia is very smart. She figured out there was no way the hotel was losing money. She knew someone was taking some of the income. She figured it had to be me since I was in charge of the hotel's finances. After I got rid of Maria, she figured I had something to do with her death and told me I had better split the money with her if I wanted her to keep quiet. I told her to get lost, that she had no proof that I was taking any of the profits or that I had gotten rid of Maria. Actually I was going to bump her off next."

Natalia laughed. "I was fooling around with Souza. I knew Maria was killed with that anesthetic he always uses on his patients. He told me Yasmin was the only one who had the key to the cabinet where he kept the drug. He was going to tell the police, but he turned up dead before he could do it."

She snaked the car into the right lane to pass another slow car in the left lane and concentrated on her driving.

"I was all ready to get rid of Natalia too," Yasmin said. "But I realized she could help me get rid of Sumiko who was nosing around. I told her I'd give her enough money to get to New York if she'd kill her."

"Why are you telling that Hoofer all this stuff?"

Natalia said when the traffic had cleared enough
for her to speed up and get on the main highway
to São Paulo.

"Who is she going to tell?" Yasmin said. "She'll
be dead soon. It doesn't matter what she knows."

"When my friends call the police to tell them
I've disappeared," I said, "and the police find
out you're gone, too, don't you think they'll
come after you?"

"By the time that happens we'll be in another
car and deep in the heart of São Paulo where I
have friends," Natalia said.

"How will you get another car?" I asked. I was
trying to keep her talking so they'd forget about
throwing me out of the car.

"I have friends everywhere," she said. "It's
none of your business anyway."

My mind was racing. How was I going to get
out of this car without being shot or killed on
the highway? Not a clue. This was it. I closed my
eyes and pretended to sleep.

When I opened them we had been driving
along the highway for about an hour according
to the clock on the dashboard.

"Yasmin," I said.

"What do you want," she said.

"I've got to go to the bathroom. Could you
please stop at a gas station?"

"We're not stopping anywhere," she said.
"Hold it in."

"I'm not kidding," I said. "I'll get the seat all
wet if you don't stop."

"It's all right," Natalia said. "We can stop. I

want to get a bottle of water anyway, and we could use some gas."

"Didn't you fill up the car before we left?" Yasmin said, sounding annoyed.

"There wasn't time. When I found out what you were planning, it was too late to fill up the car."

"Oh, all right," Yasmin said, not at all pleased. "Stop at the next station."

She glared at me. "And don't get any funny ideas about getting away when we get there. I'll be right there next to you with my gun."

Her mother moaned. Yasmin turned to her, the gun still against my side.

"What is it, *mãe?*" she asked.

"Sick," her mother said holding her stomach. "Sick."

"Stop the car, Natalia," Yasmin said. "My mother is going to throw up."

Natalia cut through the lanes of traffic and stopped in the emergency lane on the right. Yasmin handed her gun to Natalia.

"Watch her while I help my mother," she said.

Natalia leaned over the front seat pointing the gun at me. "Don't even think about it," she said.

Yasmin helped her mother out of the car and led her into the wooded area next to the highway. They moved very slowly. I tried desperately to figure out a way to get out of there. I had to try. It was my only chance.

"Natalia," I said, "you don't need me anymore. I'm just a burden to you. Why don't you let me get out of the car now? You can leave me here. By the time I get back to Rio, you'll be safe in São Paulo."

"You'd like that, wouldn't you, you clever little Hoofer?" she said.

"Why not?" I asked.

"Because you know too much," she said. "We need you dead."

After about twenty minutes, Yasmin brought her mother back to the car.

Natalia looked away for a minute to make sure Yasmin could lift her mother into the backseat. I ducked down on the floor and lunged at Yasmin to knock her down on top of her mother. Natalia couldn't shoot at me without the chance of hitting one or both of them. I ran out into the lane of cars and waved my arms wildly at the automobile speeding toward me. The driver veered sharply into the next lane and pulled over to the emergency lane to stop. I ran to his car, jumped in, and said, "Quick, get me out of here. I'm being kidnapped. Get me to the nearest police station please."

The man driving the car didn't ask any questions at first. He just sped off, and I collapsed on the seat in the back.

After a short distance, he asked, "Who are you? Why were you kidnapped?" he asked.

I was relieved to hear him speak English.

"I'll explain it all to you when we get to the police," I said. "Could you get off at the next exit and find the nearest police station."

I looked out the back window and saw Natalia's car gaining on us. I could see her fierce little face through the windshield.

"Oh, hurry, they're right behind us," I said.

He accelerated the car and took the next exit. Natalia followed us. The man stopped at the small police station on the main street of the town. Natalia came up right behind us and got out of the car and ran to him.

"Oh, thank you, sir," she said. "My aunt has been having hallucinations and she thought she was being kidnapped. I'm so grateful to you for helping her. She'll be fine now. We'll get her back to the institution."

The man looked totally confused. He got out of the car and I was sure he was going to hand me over to her.

"Don't believe her," I said. "Please don't believe her. She's trying to kill me."

"Well, I . . ." he began. I'm sure he didn't know whom to believe—this well-spoken, attractive young woman driving the other car or the wild-eyed, disheveled woman he picked up in the middle of the highway.

He looked like he was just about to hand me over to Natalia so I jumped out of the car and ran into the police station.

The police officer behind the desk stood up. I must have been a mess. Hair falling in my eyes, a crazy look on my face, a desperate person.

He said something to me in Portuguese.

"Do you speak English?" I said

"Yes, senhora," he said.

"Help me," I said. "I've been kidnapped by that woman out there."

"Kidnapped?" he said. "Senhora . . ."

"Oh, please, senhor, call the chief of police in Rio. Senhor Pereira. He knows me. He knows they took me out of there. He must be looking for me now."

"Senhor Pereira, the chief of police in Rio?" he asked.

"Yes, yes, do you know him?" I said.

"I know who he is," the police officer said. "I've never met him."

Natalia and Yasmin burst into the station. My rescuer followed them. He clearly still didn't know whom to believe.

"Thank God you're all right," Natalia said to me, putting her arms around me. "We were so worried." She looked like the most respectable person on earth, concerned about her beloved aunt who had gone off her rocker.

There was a rapid exchange in Portuguese between Natalia, the man who saved me and the police officer.

The police officer said to me in English, "I think you'd better go with your niece. She'll take good care of you." I couldn't blame him. I would have believed her too.

I clung to his desk. "Just do one thing for me please, Officer. Call Chief Pereira. Please. I beg you. It will only take a minute."

He hesitated, looking back and forth between Natalia and me.

"She was running out on the highway," the man in the car said. "I believed what she told me."

The police officer hesitated once more and then picked up the phone. "It won't hurt to call Pereira," he said.

"Chief Pereira," he said after a moment. "Police officer Fernandes calling."

He waited a couple of seconds and then told my story to the chief.

"Yes. She's with two women," he said.

He opened the door of the station and gave the chief the license plate number on Natalia's car.

"I understand, sir." he said. "We'll hold them here for you."

Yasmin grabbed Natalia's arm and pulled her out of the station into the car. The police officer dropped the phone and ran after them, but they were too fast for him. They were in the car and headed back toward the highway before he could stop them.

He picked up the phone and told Pereira what had happened.

"Yes, sir. I'll send out my men immediately," he said. He hung up and sent out an all-points bulletin to his officers.

I fell on the floor. I had not one ounce of strength left. My rescuer and Fernandes carried me to a bench in the station. The police officer poured me a cup of coffee.

"Try to tell me what's happening here," he said. "Who are you? Who are those women? Why were they trying to kidnap you?"

I took a sip of the coffee, which revived me a

little. "They're involved in the murders at the Copacabana," I said. "You must have heard about them."

"Everyone has heard about them," he said. "It was in all the papers. Three murders in the most exclusive hotel in Rio. You mean those women had something to do with the murders?"

"Yes," I said. "I found out that they had done it. They abducted me and were using me as their hostage. I managed to jump out of their car and this man stopped for me." I looked at him and realized I hadn't ever thanked him. "I am so grateful to you, sir," I said.

"I'm just glad you're safe," he said. He obviously wanted to get out of there. "May I go?" he asked Officer Fernandes.

"Yes, you can go. But leave me your card please so we can get in touch with you later."

The man pulled out his wallet and handed the officer his business card.

"How can I ever thank you?" I asked him. "I don't even know your name."

"I'm Luis Lima. Try to stay out of trouble," he said with a smile. He shook my hand and left.

"You are very lucky, senhora," the officer said. "If that man hadn't stopped for you, you'd be dead now."

I started to shiver. "I know, I know," I said. "Do you think you'll be able to catch them?"

"I'm sure we will, senhora," he said. "Do not worry."

I didn't tell him that "worry" was my middle name.

"I have no way to get back to Rio," I said. "Did Captain Pereira say anything about sending a car for me?"

"Yes, he did," Fernandes said. "It may take a while, but someone will come. Would you like to rest for a while until they get here?"

"That sounds wonderful, Senhor Fernandes. I really need some sleep."

"If you don't mind sleeping in a jail cell, I can put you in one of those. They're actually fairly comfortable."

"I can sleep anywhere," I said. "Thank you."

He led me to a cell, put a blanket over me, and I fell asleep almost immediately.

Pat's Tip for Traveling with Friends: If you're spontaneous and she wants to plan every minute, compromise. Teach her the fun of doing something totally unplanned.

Chapter Seventeen

One More Time and I'm Out of Here!

I woke up in the backseat of a car. It was daylight. I must have slept in that jail cell all night. I remembered Officer Fernandes saying, "They're here for you, Senhora Keeler," but I was still half-asleep and let them carry me to the car. I couldn't wait to get back to the Copacabana.

I opened my eyes. I had no idea what time it was. I said to the uniformed back of the person driving, "*Bom dia*, senhor."

The driver turned around slowly, a smile on his face. "*Bom dia*, senhora."

I jumped up, startled. It was Ramon. How could it be Ramon? Where was the policeman?

"How did you . . . ? What are you doing . . . ?" I managed to say. I could not believe this.

"I got rid of the police officer who was coming to get you," he said, "and took you out of the jail."

"But how did you know where I was? I said. "Yasmin said you were back in the favela."

"I was," he said, "but Natalia called me and told me you had escaped and she needed another car. They had to abandon hers because the police were after her and Yasmin so I borrowed this one."

"Where are they?" I asked. The thought of them still at large made me shudder.

"Not far. They'll be so glad to see you again!" He laughed. "Don't even think of jumping out of the car, senhora. I'm going about eighty-five and you'll end up in little pieces in the road."

I could not imagine how I was going to get away this time. My escape valve was definitely clogged. I would have to talk my way out of this one. And fast.

"Ramon," I said, "do you really want to get mixed up with those two women again?"

"They have money for me," he said. "As soon as I get it, I'm going back to Rio. They just want you. They don't care what I do."

"I know a way you can get a lot more money than they have," I said.

"Oh, yeah," he said sarcastically. "How's that?"

"I can get you a job driving cars in New York," I said. "I know people there who are always looking for drivers. And they'll pay you a lot. You'll have a much better life in the States than back in the favelas."

"I don't believe you," he said. "You can't get me a job. Do you think I'm stupid?"

"I mean it," I said. "Just pull off the highway at the next exit and park somewhere. I'll put in a call to a friend of mine in New York. He'll tell you about a job and how much money you'll make. What can you lose?"

"You can't really do that, can you?" he asked. I could hear the doubt in his voice. There was the smallest chance that I might be able to help him.

"Try me," I said. "If you don't like what my friend says, you can just say no. If you like it, we can go right to the airport and fly to New York."

I didn't really think he would buy this at all. I didn't believe any of it myself.

He drove on in silence. As we approached the next exit, he slowed down and took the ramp into a small town and stopped in the parking lot of a restaurant.

"You better be telling the truth," he said. "Go ahead. Call. You have ten minutes."

I dialed Alex Boyer, Gini's boyfriend in New York who worked for the *New York Times*. He was brilliant and I knew he'd know what to do.

Please let him be there. Please.

He picked up right away. When I heard his familiar voice, I said, "Hello, Alex. It's Pat Keeler."

"Pat!" he said. "How are you? Is Gini all right? Is everything OK?"

"Not really, Alex," I said. "Remember you told me you needed drivers?"

"Drivers?" he said. "What are you talking about?"

"I knew you were looking for drivers," I said. "I'm here with someone who is looking for work in New York. I told him I would call you, and he said he would consider it."

"Are you in some kind of trouble, Pat?"

"Yes, that's right, Alex, very big."

"Let me talk to him," Ramon said, grabbing the phone out of my hand. "I don't trust you."

"What are you paying?" he asked Alex, his Portuguese accent very strong.

Alex must have caught on immediately and quoted some huge number.

Ramon handed the phone back to me. "Tell him OK."

"Alex, we're going to the airport in Rio now, and we'll get the next American Airlines flight to New York."

"I'll call the Rio police the minute you hang up," Alex said. "I'll tell them where you are. Hang in there, Pat."

"That's excellent," I said. "I know Ramon will be pleased."

"Call me as soon as you get to the airport," Alex said.

"Thank you, Alex," I said. "See you soon."

When I hung up, I said to Ramon, "Get to the Rio airport as fast as you can. We'll get the next plane to New York. They run every couple of hours. My friend Alex will pick us up at the airport, and you'll start right away. He said he would find you a place to stay. He said any friend of mine was a friend of his."

"I should call Yasmin and tell her what I'm doing," he said.

Oh, dear God.

"Yasmin will never let you do that," I said, taking a deep breath and praying I could convince him not to call her. "You know too much about what she has done. Better get to the airport and out of Brazil as fast as you can."

"It will only take a minute," he said. He dialed a number and waited.

"Yasmin? It's Ramon." He continued the conversation in Portuguese, and I assumed he was telling her about my plan to take him to New York to a fabulous new job. My heart sank. I knew what her reaction would be.

Her answer was so loud I could hear it standing next to him. A long rapid fire of Portuguese words shot through the phone. I was sure she was telling him not to go to New York with me.

When he hung up he glared at me. "I almost fell for it," he said. "I don't know why I thought I could trust you. I think the police will be waiting for me at the airport. We're going in the opposite direction. I'm taking you to Yasmin. She'll know what to do with you. Don't try any more tricks, senhora."

"Ramon," I said, desperately trying to talk him into believing me. I knew it was a lost cause. Yasmin had put the fear of God into him. "Ramon, there won't be any police at the airport. My friend has a job waiting for you. It pays a lot. If you stay here, you'll get a little money, but nothing like you can make in New York."

"How did you think I could get on that plane without a passport?" he asked. I was afraid he'd think of that.

"I'd tell them you are my assistant and that you would fly on my passport. People do it all the time." Who would believe that? Certainly not me. And as it turned out, not Ramon either.

"I'm not that stupid," he said. "I'd be in jail before I finished checking in at the airport. We're going to meet Yasmin—now!"

He started the car and accelerated to a high speed before I could get the door open and escape. He would have caught me anyway. He was a large, strong man who would have intercepted me in no time. I'd have to think of something else.

We sped along the highway. There didn't seem to be much hope. Once we met Yasmin and Natalia, they'd be sure to get rid of me this time. Somehow, I would have to get away from Ramon before we got there.

"How much farther, Ramon?" I asked.

"Not far. Another twenty minutes, maybe," he said.

Twenty minutes. We were going at least eighty miles an hour. I couldn't jump out of the car. I closed my eyes.

Then I heard a sound that was sweeter than

the song of angels, even sweeter than a cat's meow. A police siren. A siren that got louder and louder as it caught up with us. Ramon speeded up even more. I looked out the back window. The police car was right on our tail. I could see the officer's face grimly intent on keeping pace with Ramon. I opened my purse and pulled out a piece of paper and scrawled HELP across it. I held it up to the window. *Please let that policeman know at least this much English.*

He didn't change expression or acknowledge my note, so I had no way of knowing whether he understood my message. I made a scared face and put my hands together in prayer mode so he would know I was asking for help. I hoped. He didn't respond, but I knew he was concentrating on catching up to Ramon.

Ramon swerved suddenly and took the next exit ramp. The police car was right behind him. The turn was so abrupt I fell on the floor of the car. I got back on the seat and saw that we were in another small town with narrow winding streets, forcing Ramon to slow down. When he did, the police car sped up and drove in front of him so he had to stop.

The officer, his face angry, rapped on the window. Ramon pulled out a gun. Before he could fire a shot, I hit his hand with my bag as hard as I could. He dropped the gun, the policeman yanked open the door, and grabbed Ramon and handcuffed him.

"Oh, Officer," I said. "Help me."

He kept his gun pointed at Ramon and said something to me in Portuguese.

I remembered Lucas's language lesson.

"Você fala inglês, senhor?" I said, pretty sure it meant "Do you speak English?"

"A little bit, senhora," he said. "Who are you?"

"Pat Keeler. American. This man kidnapped me."

"Kidnapped?" the officer said, looking bewildered.

"Call Captain Pereira in Rio," I said, using the universal sign for making a phone call—two fingers next to the ear.

"Ah," he said. "Captain Pereira. I call."

I nodded vigorously and smiled. *"Sim,"* I said, trying to pronounce it correctly, sort of like "sing" in English. "Yes."

Still watching Ramon who was bent over the hood of the car, his hands handcuffed behind him, the officer dialed a number and after a minute, said, "Senhor Pereira?" Then he spieled off a whole story in Portuguese about the present situation. He looked at me, said *"Sim"* into the phone, and then listened to Pereira's answer.

When he hung up, he said, "Pereira comes."

"Oh, thank goodness," I said. I tried to tell him about Yasmin and Natalia, but he couldn't understand me. I knew it would be at least an hour before Pereira could get here and by then, my two murderesses would be long gone. They would know something was wrong when Ramon didn't show up and they couldn't reach him.

How could I get Ramon to lead this officer to his friends?

My only hope was that when Yasmin called him, the policeman could force Ramon at gunpoint to find out where she was, and the officer would capture them. But how could I explain this to the policeman?

I couldn't. I pulled out my own phone and called Pereira. I had him on speed dial since my night in the favelas. He answered right away. I explained what I was trying to do. He asked to speak to the local police officer again and told him my plan. The police officer nodded, said, "*Sim, sim,*" and hung up.

Now all we had to do was wait for Ramon's phone to ring. I reached into the car and retrieved it from the front seat where Ramon had left it.

Nothing happened. Five minutes, ten minutes. Then the ring.

The police officer, whose name tag identified him as Joao Silva, put the gun against Ramon's head and told him to say hello and ask for their location.

"*Alo,*" Ramon said into the phone. The policeman clicked off the safety on the gun. Ramon, I hoped, asked his listener for their location then handed the phone to Officer Silva. Silva listened, said nothing, then hung up.

Silva said to me, "I call other police." He made another call, his gun still against Ramon's head.

Within minutes, several police cars joined our

officer's car. He handed Ramon over to two of them who took him away, I hoped forever.

Officer Silva motioned to one of the other policemen. "He speak English," he said to me. He explained what I was doing there briefly to the other officer and I heard the word *Pereira* in there.

"Senhora," Silva said. "He take care of you. My men. I. We get bad girls."

I almost laughed. It was so funny to me to hear Yasmin and Natalia, the two most dangerous women I'd ever met in my life, two killers, called "bad girls," as if they had not done their homework the night before.

"My prayers go with you," I said. I don't know whether he understood me or not, but he shook my hand and got back in his car. The others lined up behind him. *Let them get those two,* I prayed. I seemed to be talking to God a lot lately for a not-so-religious person.

The English-speaking policeman said, "Come, senhora, I will take you to a safe place to wait for Captain Pereira. Perhaps you would like something to eat. Or some tea or coffee?"

"Oh, thank you," I said. "I would like that very much."

He took my arm and led me to a coffee shop nearby. "My name is Caio Tiago," he said. I ordered an omelet and some tea. He sat down beside me and said, "You're American, aren't you?" I nodded. "My mother is American," he said.

"I wondered how you spoke English so well," I said.

"As you can imagine, I'm very fond of Americans," he said. "Tell me how you got mixed up in all this. What are you doing getting kidnapped in the middle of Brazil? A nice woman like you."

I tried to explain the whole mess to him, but it was such a weird and mixed-up story that I despaired of his understanding half of it.

"You must hate Brazil after going through all of that," he said.

"I don't exactly hate it," I said. "But I must admit I won't mind going home tomorrow. I live in a little town in New Jersey and most people there just die of natural causes."

He laughed. "Where in New Jersey?" he asked.

"Champlain," I said. "It's a very small town."

"My mother grew up in Madison," he said. "Have you ever heard of it?"

"It's practically next door," I said. "Tell your mother she raised a very nice man."

He smiled. "She'd love to meet you," he said. "I'm sorry you won't be here longer."

"I'd love to meet her too," I said. "But I need to get back to Rio. My friends probably think I'm dead."

"Why don't you call them?" he said.

I was in such a state I hadn't even thought of calling Tina and telling her I was all right. I assumed Pereira would have told her, but I thought I'd better make sure.

Tina answered on the first ring.

"Pat!" she said, her voice betraying her worry.

"Where are you? Are you all right? Oh, sweetie, we've been frantic."

"You'll never believe what happened," I said. "I don't even believe it myself. Tina, I'm in the middle of nowhere, in some little town between Rio and São Paulo, talking to a nice police officer with an American mother – from Madison!"

I knew I was babbling on without making much sense, but I couldn't help it.

"How are you getting back here?" Tina asked.

"Pereira is coming to get me and Yasmin and Natalia. If they don't get away again. Those two are the slipperiest weasels I've ever met."

"Well, get back here as soon as you can," she said. "We miss you."

"Don't worry," I said. "I'll be there as fast as I can."

"Bye, hon," she said. "See you soon."

I hung up and my officer friend patted my hand.

He told me more about his mother. How she had come to Rio for Carnaval when she was young, met his father, fell in love, and has lived in Brazil ever since. I told him about Denise and David. Before I knew it, we had talked for a couple of hours and a police car pulled up outside the café. It was Chief Pereira. He grabbed my hand when he came in and then, surprisingly, gave me a hug. I just wasn't suspecting a hug from the Chief of Police somehow.

"Thank heavens you're all right, senhora," he said.

"I don't think I can take one more kidnapping, Captain Pereira," I said. "Have you heard whether Officer Silva and his colleagues have captured Yasmin?"

"I haven't heard yet," he said. "But I'm sure I will any minute. They can't get away this time."

"I've heard that so many times before, I'm beginning to think they'll never be caught." I said.

"This time we know where they are. As soon as I hear that they've been captured, I'll take you back to Rio."

I ordered another cup of tea.

Pereira's phone rang. "This is it," he said to me. *"Olá."*

He listened for what seemed forever, his face impassive. Why was it taking so long for them to tell him Yasmin and Natalia were caught and in jail? Because I always expect the worst, I held my breath when Pereira hung up.

"What?" I said.

He took my hand again. "Senhora, something unexpected, I'm afraid."

I covered my face with my hands. I cannot stand this. "Tell me," I said.

"Silva's men captured Yasmin and Natalia and they were taking them back to Rio to jail, when Yasmin's mother had a heart attack. They rushed her to the hospital. Yasmin pleaded with the officer to let her stay with her mother. There was so much confusion, they let her accompany her mother to the emergency room. Another car took Natalia back to Rio."

I knew what he was going to say next.

"Yasmin got away, didn't she?" I asked.

"I'm afraid so," he said. "They made the mistake of leaving her alone in the hospital room with her mother. They didn't think she would leave when her mother was in critical condition. But they underestimated Yasmin. In the few minutes they left the room, she managed to put on a hospital gown and a face mask and slip out of the hospital."

"Do you think she'll go back to Rio?" I asked. I dreaded his answer.

"I'm afraid so, senhora," he said. "She has friends in the favelas and they'll hide her there. The police are afraid to go in there anyway."

I couldn't speak. The thought that she was free and could find me was too much.

Pereira read my mind. He could see the fear on my face. "But we will guard you every minute, senhora. And you're leaving tomorrow. She can't get you again."

I didn't believe him. "Could we go back to the hotel now, please, Captain Pereira? I need to be with my friends."

He took my hand. "Come. I'll take you there now."

I said good-bye to Tiago. "I will pray for you, senhora," he said.

"Say hello to your mother for me," I said. "And come see me if you ever come to New Jersey."

He kissed me on both cheeks and I left with Pereira.

Pat's Tip for Traveling with Friends: There's nothing wrong with each of you going your separate way once in a while. You're not joined at the hip.

Chapter Eighteen

God's Gift

When we got back to the hotel, it was late in the afternoon. My friends were waiting outside. I stumbled out of Chief Pereira's car and into a group hug from all my Hoofers.

"Thank God you're all right," Mary Louise said.

"What happened?" Gini said.

"You look terrible," Janice said.

"Come have tea," Tina said.

"I've had enough tea to last me a lifetime," I said. "I need a drink."

"Oh, Pat, are you sure?" Tina said. Her pretty face showed concern for my jumping off the wagon.

"It's just temporary, Tina," I said. "Don't worry. One caipirinha won't make me into a drinker again."

"She looks like she needs that drink," Janice said. "Come on, Pat."

They led me into the Piano Bar, and I ordered a caipirinha.

"We thought you were safe," Gini said. "In your own room. Fast asleep. The next minute you were in some police station halfway between here and São Paulo. I think we need to put you on a leash."

"Would you please?" I said.

"Nobody has told us anything," Tina said. "We thought Yasmin was the killer. Then Pereira said you had been kidnapped by Natalia and Yasmin. Natalia! That ditzy little redhead who flibbets around here. Natalia. I couldn't believe it."

"And Pereira said something about Ramon," Gini said. "Our helpful, good driver Ramon. Always smiling, always so friendly. Pereira said that he grabbed you in the police station and was taking you to meet Yasmin and Natalia."

"And Yasmin's mother," I said. "Don't forget her. It was because of her getting sick that I got away from them the first two times. Unfortunately it was her heart attack that allowed Yasmin to escape again."

"What do you mean 'escape again'?" Gini asked. "Go back. How did you get away from Ramon? Alex called me and said you phoned him and arranged for Ramon to go to the airport with you to fly to New York and then the police would arrest him at the airport. He promised Ramon lots of money to be a driver in New York or something."

"Right," I said. "I thought it was all set. Alex was terrific, of course. He understood that I was in trouble and managed to con Ramon into agreeing to come to New York to drive for some huge amount of money."

"So what happened?" Gini asked.

"We were about to go to the airport when Ramon decided he'd better call Yasmin. That was the end of that plan. She yelled at him that it was a trick and that he should bring me to them immediately."

"What did you do?" Tina asked. "Obviously you got away. How did you do it?"

"Believe me," I said, "I was totally out of ideas. It was Ramon who made the mistake that caught him."

"How?" Mary Louise asked.

"He drove about eighty-five miles an hour so I couldn't jump out of the car. I had just about decided there was nothing I could do. Then, all of a sudden, I heard a police siren and a police car was chasing him—for speeding, I guess. I don't know why, but I didn't ask any questions. Ramon turned off the highway into this little town and the policeman got him."

"So then what?" Janice asked.

"The policeman—a lovely man—Officer Silva—wanted to help me but he didn't speak much English, so I tried to explain to him that

I had been kidnapped and Ramon knew where these two murderesses were and he had to find them and—"

"He didn't understand you," Gini said.

"Right."

"What did you do?"

"I realized I should call Chief Pereira here and he would explain the whole thing to Senhor Silva in Portuguese," I said. I looked at the Chief with gratitude. "He did, and I thought Yasmin and Natalia would finally be caught. Well, they were caught. But Yasmin got away. Of course she got away."

"How did she do that?" Tina asked.

"Yasmin's mother, the same mother who saved me before with her illness, was Yasmin's escape this time. She had a heart attack and the police let Yasmin go to the emergency room with her mother. They left her alone for a short time and she got away. Chief Pereira thinks she probably will go to the favelas where her friends will hide her. The same favelas where she almost killed me. It's a good thing we're leaving tomorrow or she might manage to succeed this time."

Tina put her arm around me. "You're safe now, hon. She'll never get to you again. There are police all over the hotel. We're with you all the time."

I knew I'd never feel safe until I was back in New Jersey and Yasmin was locked up in some jail for a long, long time.

The waiter brought my caipirinha. I could feel my friends' eyes on me. I knew they were afraid I would start drinking again. They all loved me a lot. I took a sip of the caipirinha and it didn't do a thing for me. I thought I would get that same lift, that same relaxation I always got before when I reached for a drink. But now, nothing. I motioned to the waiter and asked for a ginger ale instead. He took the caipirinha back.

I could see the smiles on the faces of all my drinking friends. They were happy for me. They're always glad when something good happens to me. As I am for them.

"I still don't know how you got through all that," Gini said.

"I don't either, Gini," I said. "I just kept praying for help."

"Sometimes I think God needs a hearing aid," Gini said. "How come He didn't hear you when Yasmin kidnapped you, then Natalia, then Ramon?"

I laughed. Gini always makes me laugh. She could make me laugh if the two of us were stranded on some desert island with only bananas to eat.

"He must have been busy," I said. "But look, I'm here. What time is it anyway?" I had lost all track of time.

"It's four-thirty," Tina said. "Do you want to sleep?"

"No, thanks," I said. "I slept all night in that cell before Ramon liberated me. I'm slept out. I'm afraid if I go to sleep again I'll wake up with someone pointing a gun at me or in the backseat of a car driven by the friend of a killer. I'm never going to sleep again. I need a shower though. Gini would you mind keeping watch outside the shower door?"

"I'm not letting you out of my sight until Yasmin and Natalia are in jail for the rest of their lives," she said.

"There will be a police officer outside the door of your suite," Pereira said. "He will be with you everywhere you go."

"Not in the shower, I hope," I said.

He smiled. "Everywhere but there," he said. "I have policemen all over the hotel," he said. "I promise you you're safe."

Because I never really believe everything is all right, I still couldn't relax, no matter how much Pereira tried to reassure me.

Then I heard a sweet little meow.

Mary Louise was holding my kitten. She handed him over to me. All of a sudden, everything was fine. This baby licked my hand and nestled close to me, purring. I wanted to find a name for this perfect little creature even though I couldn't take him back home with me. There was always a chance I could come back for him when he was older.

"What shall I call him?" I asked my friends. It was good to have something else to think about besides my recent horrible experiences.

"How about 'Janeiro'?" Gini said.

"That's not quite right," I said. "Think of something else."

"Why don't you call your cat 'Gato Doce'?" Miguel said. "It means 'sweet cat' in Portuguese.

Or you could call him 'Namorado,' which means 'boyfriend.' "

"You're getting closer," I said. "But I need something else. I love his little white collar. I want something like that, but not 'white collar.' "

"How about naming him after some priest, then?" Gini said. "They wear white collars."

I just looked at her. "The day I name my cat after a priest, you can send me off to a nunnery," I said. "Think of something totally nonreligious. Something that will remind me he came to me at a time when I needed something warm and loving."

"I've got it," Tina said. "Call him Rio. That's where he's from, after all."

"That's it!" I said. "Rio is perfect. Thank you, my talented editor friend." I kissed my little cat on the top of his head and said, "Olá, Rio." He purred.

"Come on, Pat. Let's get you cleaned up and we'll have one last incredible dinner in Rio," Tina said.

"Anything where I'm surrounded by all of you," I said. "Oh, and a few hundred policemen."

The hot shower felt heavenly. I just stood there and let the water wash over me, cleaning and soothing and warming me. I wanted to stay in there forever. After about fifteen minutes I turned off the shower and wrapped myself in one of the hotel's thick, luxurious towels. I came into the

main part of the suite, where Gini was all dressed
and ready for dinner.

"Go ahead," I said to her. "I'll be down in a
minute. Nothing can happen to me now. There's
an officer just outside the door. I'll be fine."

"Are you sure?" Gini said. "I don't want to
leave you if you have any qualms at all about
being left alone here."

"I'm fine, Gini, thanks."

She left, and I pulled out a long white dress
with a deep V-neck I had been saving to wear on
our last night at the Copacabana. That with a
turquoise necklace and earrings would make
me feel beautiful.

There was a knock on the door and the police
officer stuck his head in.

"Excuse me, senhora. The maid is here to put
fresh towels in the bathroom. Is it all right to let
her in?"

"Certainly, Officer," I said. "I'm about to go
downstairs anyway."

The policeman opened the door and a gray-
haired, plain-faced maid came through the door
with a pile of towels.

I sat down in front of the dressing table and
started to apply my Chanel lipstick, the reddish
pink one that is my favorite. As I looked in the
mirror, I saw another face in back of me. Yasmin. Yasmin in a gray wig, no makeup, maid's
uniform, holding a gun. I jumped up.

"Stay right where you are, sweetheart," that
familiar voice said. "You're not going anywhere
except with me. I need you as a hostage to get

back to that hospital to get my mother's body. I want to bring her back home to bury her. And you're going to help me."

"How do you think you're going to get out of this hotel?" I asked. "There are police everywhere. They're all looking for you."

"Right. They're looking for me, but they won't even give a second glance to a maid. Maids are invisible. No one really knows what they look like. I walked in here right by that policeman guarding you. I'm taking you out of here in the laundry cart. One peep out of you and I'll shoot you even if they catch me afterward. Understand?"

I nodded. This could not be happening again. I didn't believe it.

She pulled the cart into the room and dumped out all the towels and sheets and told me to get in.

I had one foot in the cart when the door to our suite opened and Gini came in. Without realizing what was happening, she said, "Forgot my camera, Pat. I want to get some shots of . . . Hey, what's going on here?"

"Watch out, Gini, she's got a gun," I yelled.

Gini, whose reactions are faster than a speeding bullet, reached for the cart and shoved it with all her might into Yasmin. I fell into the cart. Yasmin's gun went off before she fell on the floor, but she didn't hit me. At the first sound of the gunshot, the room was filled with police officers who grabbed Yasmin, took away her gun, handcuffed her and dragged her out of the room.

Pereira ran into the suite.

"Senhora, senhora, are you all right?"

I slumped inside the laundry cart, my face in my hands, my beautiful white dress torn on the side. I couldn't speak.

Gini jumped in the cart next to me and held me while I tried to stop shaking. "It's over, Pat, it's over," she said. "She won't get away this time."

When I could speak, I said, "She always managed to escape before."

"Not this time, senhora," Pereira said. "She's going directly to jail this time. No more hospital visits or any other kind of visits for her."

"I just want to go home. Away from here."

"Think you're up for one last incredible dinner at this hotel?" Gini asked. "Miguel invited us to a tasting dinner prepared by his five-star chef."

"I am *so* not hungry, Gini," I said. "I don't think I'll ever be hungry again."

"You don't have to eat, but just come to be with us and to see the presentation. Should be spectacular. Wouldn't be any fun without you."

"OK," I said, my heart not in this dinner at all. "I have to change my dress. My favorite dress. It's torn."

"You always look gorgeous whatever you wear," Gini said.

I certainly didn't feel gorgeous, but I wasn't going to disappoint these friends.

I climbed out of that horrible laundry cart and changed into my light blue dress with the little white stars around the top, my ivory necklace and earrings. Gini stayed with me the whole time, just in case any more unwelcome guests popped into the room.

When we went downstairs to the beautiful Cipriani Restaurant, Miguel bowed when he saw me and kissed my hand. "I have a special treat for you this evening, senhora," he said. "I hope you will like it."

I managed a small smile. "Of course I will, Senhor Ortega."

My other Hoofers were waiting for us. They were dressed to kill, each one more beautiful than the other. They all gathered me up into a group hug and gently led me into a seat at the table in this lovely restaurant.

Chapter Nineteen

Travel Tips for Rio

Soft music played in the background. White tablecloths, pale yellow roses, gleaming silver brought out the quiet elegance of the Cipriani Restaurant. Almost every table in the dining room was filled with formally dressed guests talking in low voices, obviously delighted to be in this famous hotel in their poshest restaurant. There were a few sloppily dressed Americans, but I tried to turn off my critical button and accept them the way they were. Some American men hate wearing starched shirts and ties and jackets on vacation. It was a fact of life.

Tina tapped on her glass to get our attention.

"Here's to our Pat," she said. "She is truly our heroine on this trip. How she got through all she did, I'll never know. But we want her to know how much we love her." She raised her glass of champagne and said, "To Pat!"

All my friends, my trusty, loving, loyal friends

who are always there for me, no matter what, raised their glasses and said, "To Pat!" in unison.

"I love you all," I said, raising my glass of co-conut water and lime juice.

Miguel applauded as he approached our table, followed by Luiz, the genial, genius chef who produced miracles in his kitchen every day.

"Luiz will tell you what he has prepared for your tasting menu," Miguel said. "Enjoy."

"*Boa tarde,* senhoras," Luiz said. "I have prepared for you this evening my specialties, and I hope you will come back to see us again soon."

Not bloody likely in this lifetime, I thought, but listened to his description of our tasting menu.

"First we start off with puff pastry and sesame crusted taleggio cheese with truffled mushrooms. Then, linguini with lobster, dill, and cherry tomatoes. Next, for your pleasure, a tuna mignon and foie gras with asparagus and Marsala wine reduction. Then my pièce de résistance, if I do say so myself, my ossobuco in gremola with saffron risotto. Finally, my eggplant gnocchi in tomato and basil sauce."

I was exhausted just listening to this list.

Luiz saw the look on our faces. "You understand, lovely senhoras, you will only have a small portion of each of these things. I tried to give you a wide selection of tastes and textures so you will find a surprise in each one."

"We are eagerly waiting your specialties, Luiz," Tina said. "Bring them on!"

Luiz's handsome face beamed with pleasure

at her words, and he waved and went back to his kitchen.

"I'll never be able to eat all that," I said. "I'm full already."

"It's called a tasting menu for a reason," Gini said. "The main purpose of all this is to excite our palates, present us with food we'll never get anywhere else. Relax, Pat. Stop worrying. Just eat what you feel like eating. You'll love this."

I realized old worrywart Pat was back. I took a deep breath and let go of everything but the anticipation of a wonderful meal with my best friends in the world.

Tina tapped on her glass again. "OK, gang," she said. "While we wait for the first course, how about helping me out with some travel tips for my honeymooners who are coming to Rio. I've got the most important one which is, 'Don't wander around by yourself at night. There are muggers everywhere.'"

"Right," Gini said. "Take someone like Mateus along with you."

"Even during the day, you should be careful," Mary Louise said. "Remember, they told us to wear our purses across our chests, not hanging down over our shoulders."

"Everybody knows you have to be careful in Rio," Tina said. "But I need some more upbeat tips for my honeymooners."

"They should check out the samba clubs," Janice said. "They're incredible. Great music, dancing, moving, moving, moving. You should tell them that they give you a card when you go in, which you should guard with your life. Whenever you order anything, they punch the amount on your card. If you lose the card they charge you some outrageous amount. So hang on to your card. Oh, and make sure the man you're with doesn't have another wife hidden away somewhere."

"That's really good, Jan," Tina said. "What else?"

"You should probably tell them the best time of year to go to Rio," I said. "I was talking to Yasmin about that—this was before I found out she was a murderer—and she said you should come here between May and October. That's their winter, believe it or not. The temperature during the day is in the upper seventies and in the fifties at night so it's really comfortable walking around. From January to March it's hot, hot, hot—often in the hundreds. Carnaval is in February and your honeymooners might want to come for that. It lasts four days—parties, music, and fun—but bring your lightest clothes. Oh, and don't come here in December because it rains all the time, often days at a time."

"Thanks, Pat," Tina said. "That's so useful."

"Not to be a worrywart or anything," Mary Louise said. "But . . ."

"That's my job," I said. "However, I'll let you take over temporarily."

Mary Louise laughed. "I'll never be as good at it as you are," she said. "But, Tina, I think you should warn your readers about getting money here. I had to try several ATMs before I found one that would give me dollars with my bank card. When I tried to exchange my dollars for real in banks, the rate was abysmal. Finally someone told me to go to a *cambio* where the rates are fairly decent."

"That reminds me," Gini said. "Another tip about ATMs. They're closed between ten at night and six in the morning. Remember that night I went out to take pictures after we danced? I started to go to an ATM and Mateus said, 'They're closed now until morning.' So I just used the little cash I had with me. They tell you not to have a lot of money on you at any time anyway."

I started to add Yasmin's tip about bargaining when Miguel himself brought our first dish, the puff pastry with taleggio cheese and truffled mushrooms. One bite and I was in heaven. I had never tasted taleggio cheese before. It had a funny smell but it had a lovely fruity taste that went perfectly with the mushrooms.

We nibbled away. Luiz was true to his word. The portion was small and just the right amount since we still had four more tasting courses to go.

"What did you start to say, Pat?" Tina asked when the waiter had cleared away the dishes. "Something about shopping?"

I started to answer her when the waiter appeared with our next course, which was even better than the one before—linguini with lobster, dill and cherry tomatoes.

"Oh Tina," Mary Louise said after her first bite. "Isn't there some way we can stay here another day, or week, or . . ."

"Wish we could, Wheezie," Tina said. "But what would George do without you?"

"Who cares?" she said, taking another bite and closing her eyes in ecstasy.

"Go ahead, Pat," Tina said. "What else did you find out about shopping?"

"Yasmin also told me it's OK to bargain in those street shops," I said. "But if you go into the regular stores in the mall, you do not bargain. That's insulting. They're like our stores. You pay whatever is on the price tag. But the little boutiques on the street are fair game."

"Glad she was so helpful before she kidnapped you and tried to murder you," Gini said.

I tensed up. I could see Yasmin with that syringe in her hands, filling it with an anesthetic that would kill me. I shut my eyes and tried to blot out that memory.

"Gini, sometimes you have no sense," Tina said, reaching over to put her hand on mine. "Are you all right, Pat?"

"Sort of," I said.

"Oh, Pat, I'm so sorry," Gini said. "I didn't mean to—"

"I know you didn't, Gini," I said. "It's just that it's so recent, it still scares me to death." I shook myself and came back to the present.

"She also gave me some useful phone numbers you might want to include in the article, Tina," I said.

"What are they?" she said.

"In case you're robbed, you call 190 for the police. If you need an ambulance, you dial 192, and if you catch on fire, call 193. I think I'll have those numbers tattooed on my arm."

"I'll definitely include the police number in the article," Tina said, "but I don't want to make them think they'll need an ambulance or the fire department on their honeymoon. I'm not even sure about the police number. I don't want to emphasize the dangerous part of coming to Rio, even though everyone mentions it when you say you're coming here."

"Tell them to call me," I said, "if they need convincing."

"Everyone else will tell them that, so you probably don't have to," Mary Louise said.

"You're right," Tina said. "I'll think about it. What else should we tell our honeymooners? Anything about the beaches? That's the big attraction here."

"Something I found out that seems odd," Janice said. "You can wear practically no bathing suit at all—you know, just a thong and a miniscule bra, but you can't go topless. I think there's one nude beach in Rio, but all the other beaches require tops. If your honeymooners are coming here in one hundred degree heat, the bride might be tempted to take off her bra. I certainly would. But it's definitely frowned on."

"Good to know, Jan," Tina said. "When you see what the women wear here, you'd certainly think topless was OK. Anything else I should put in this article?"

"You might want to tell them to learn some Portuguese words and phrases before they come,"

Mary Louise said. "I've been surprised at how few people speak English here. They do in the big stores, of course, but in the little shops and walking around, they don't really understand you. I draw pictures on my iPad or wave my arms around, or point to things and make a face like I want to know how much it costs, but it would be good to learn some of those phrases Lucas taught us. Before I came here, I thought I could use the few Spanish words I know, but Portuguese is way different."

"I'm glad you reminded me of that," Tina said. "That's really important. I think I have the most crucial for the article. I'll tell them about the four zones in the city: central, where the theater and museum of fine arts are, the upscale south zone where our Copacabana, the Ipanema, Leblon are, plus Sugar Loaf and Corcovado, the north zone where the Maracaña Stadium and the zoo are, and the west zone, which is suburban and where the 2016 Olympics will be."

The waiter brought our next course, the tuna mignon and foie gras with asparagus.

"Enough shop talk," Tina said. "Let's just concentrate on this made-in-heaven food and think about where we want to go next."

We all made suggestions in between bites of this unbelievable fish with foie gras—what an ingenious combination. *Must have it at my next dinner party,* I thought. Yeah, right.

"You mean, we now get to choose where we want to dance?" Mary Louise asked, as surprised as the rest of us.

"Not bad, huh?" Tina said, looking pleased. "I've been getting lots of offers for us lately."

"I'm amazed that anyone would want to hire us, considering the body count when we leave," I said. I couldn't help it. After all, I was almost in that last body count.

"It gives us a certain excitement value," Tina said. "I know. It's weird, but our names are beginning to bring in more customers because people think they might end up on the front page of the newspaper."

"Or at least in the obituary section," Gini said, making us laugh.

"Come on, guys," Tina said. "Where shall we go next?"

"What are our choices?" Janice asked. "Couldn't we go someplace closer to home? I'm trying to work on that book about the Gypsy Robes with my daughter Sandy, and we keep dancing whole continents away."

"What would you say about dancing in New York City?" Tina asked.

We all talked at once.

"Perfect!" Gini said. "I could spend some time with Alex. I miss him."

"George would be thrilled," Mary Louise said about her husband, who always complained when she went so far away on our gigs.

"And I could finally get a chance to see more of Tom," Janice said. "I think I like him a lot but haven't really had a chance to find out."

"Denise could stop holding her breath that I'll end up dead," I said.

"And Peter and I might actually find a few minutes to get married," Tina said.

"Where would we dance?" I asked.

Before Tina could answer me, the waiter brought what Luiz called his pièce de résistance—the ossobuco with saffron risotto. I found out ossobuco is a veal shank simmered in gremola. One bite and I didn't care where we would dance in New York. It was perfection.

But Gini had to know, of course.

"Where in New York, Tina?" she said. "Tell us."

"You won't believe this," Tina said, "but somebody at Radio City Music Hall read about our Paris adventure and invited us to dance with the Rockettes in their Christmas show!"

"The Rockettes," Janice said. "You can't mean it. They're the best in the world. How can we dance with them?"

"Their manager thought it would be fun if we came out on the stage before they did, dressed like the Rockettes, and started dancing, and then were joined by all the real Rockettes who'd include us dancing to Christmas songs."

"But nobody ever dances with the Rockettes," Gini said.

"Well, we will," Tina said. "That is, if you guys want to do it."

We all talked at once, bubbling over with enthusiasm at the idea of actually being on the same stage as the Rockettes.

"It's lots of work, gang," Tina said. "They rehearse like crazy. That's why they're always perfect."

"So we'll be in New York a lot," Gini said, the enthusiasm in her voice coming through loud and clear. "We'll get to do Christmas in New York."

"You wouldn't mean you and Alex by 'we' would you, Gini?" Tina said, smiling at the look on Gini's face.

"Noooo," she said, smiling back. "Can't wait to tell him. Did you say yes to this?"

"Not yet. I wanted to see if you guys were up for this."

"We're way up," Janice said. "This will be the most fun ever. Wait till I tell Tom we're dancing with the Rockettes."

I couldn't wait to tell Denise and David I would be taking them to all kinds of Christmas stuff, including the lighting of the tree in Rockefeller Center and ice skating in their rink.

"I'll sign us up when we get home," Tina said.

Luiz appeared at our table. "How was everything, ladies?" he asked.

We all exploded with praise for his food and how exquisite it was.

"Here is your final treat," he said as the waiter served us his eggplant gnocchi in tomato and basil sauce. "If you still have room, I'd like to bring you the perfect dessert to end your meal."

A genteel groan came out of all our mouths. Where would we ever put dessert?

When we finished the eggplant delight, Luiz appeared, a big smile on his face.

"Do not worry, senhora," Luiz said. "I am bringing you a coconut white chocolate mousse. Light, sweet, and delicious." He clapped his hands and the waiter glided up to our table with sherbert glasses filled with white mousse. He was right. It was indeed the perfect ending to this incredible dinner.

"We want to thank you, Luiz," Tina said, "for this amazing meal. Every mouthful was a delight."

"My pleasure, senhora," he said and motioned for the waiter to bring espressos to finish off this evening.

When he left, Tina said, "So long, Rio. Hello, New York." We all raised our glasses in a toast to our favorite city in the world, our own helluva town, New York.

Want to celebrate Christmas in New York with us?

Keep reading to enjoy a preview excerpt from
the next Happy Hoofers mystery
HIGH KICKS, HOT CHOCOLATE,
AND HOMICIDE
Coming soon from
Kensington Publishing Corp.

Chapter One

Rock On, Rockettes

"**W**hat do you mean you're going to dance with the Rockettes?" George said, buttering his croissant and holding out his cup for more coffee.

"It's true," I said. "We're going to be part of their Christmas show."

"But they're professionals," he said.

"So are we, George," I said. "People pay us to dance. That makes us professionals."

"Mary Louise, you're a housewife," he said. "Your job is here, taking care of this house. Taking care of me."

I looked at this man I'd been married to for thirty years and wondered if he knew me at all. I had been dancing on cruise ships and trains and in hotels for the past couple of years with my friends Tina, Janice, Gini, and Pat. We call ourselves the Happy Hoofers. Our names have been all over the TV and newspapers because of a few murders here and there. We are really good dancers, and Tina, our leader, got more offers for jobs than we could accept.

Did I still love George? Sometimes I wasn't sure. I thought I was in love with Mike Parnell, the doctor I met when we danced on a luxury train in northern Spain last year. His wife had died two years before, and he was lost without her. I have the same dark hair and blue eyes she had, and he fell in love with me. I tried not to love him back, but during that trip I was ready to leave George for him. Mike was so much fun, so interesting, so good to me.

That was the part that got me, I think. He was always thinking of me and what would make me happy. George was always thinking of how I could make him happy. I tried to excuse him by reminding myself that he had his own law practice in New Jersey, that he was overworked and tired a lot of the time. Then I thought of Mike, an obstetrician, and pictured him delivering babies at all hours of the night. He still put me first. *Let it go. Mary Louise, let it go*, I told myself.

My cell rang. It was Tina Powell—travel editor of *Perfect Bride* magazine, and the leader of our Happy Hoofers troupe. We've been friends forever since the days we worked at *Redbook* magazine together and traveled across the country in a beat-up old car.

"Hi, Weezie," she said. Only my closest friends are allowed to call me that. "Ready to meet the Rockettes? We're supposed to show up at Radio City this morning for a backstage tour. Peter's going to drive us into the city. Can you believe

we're going to dance with them? The Rockettes!"

"No, I don't believe it," I said. "Tell me again
why they're letting us do this."

"Just to have something different this year.
We're only going to be on for a brief part of
their whole show. We're dancing to 'Santa Claus
Is Coming to Town,' and we're wearing very
short Santa outfits with Santa hats. We come out
on the stage alone and then all the Rockettes
join us."

"It's incredible, Tina. What time are we leaving?"

"We'll pick you up at nine. Oh, and bring
your tap shoes."

"We're going to dance this morning?"

"I think they want to see how much training
we need."

"I can tell them," I said. "A lot."

"See you at nine, hon," Tina said and hung up.

The idea of performing with the Rockettes
on the stage of Radio City was so exciting, I
practically danced to the sink with the breakfast
dishes.

"You're going into the city today?" George
asked. "I thought you were going to get the car
washed."

"Oh, George, I can do that anytime," I said.
"This is a chance to meet the Rockettes. Tina
thought we might get the chance to dance a little today, but she wasn't sure."

I rinsed off the plates and juice glasses and
stuck them in the dishwasher.

"Well, I hope you don't plan to spend much time in the city." George said. "There's a lot to do around here with Christmas coming."

"It's only October," I said, my happy mood disappearing down the sink. "I don't even have to think about shopping and the tree and all that until December. You should be glad I'm not in Thailand or someplace like that. I'll only be across the river in New York."

"Just be sure you're back here in time for dinner," he said and rattled his *New York Times* noisily.

Maybe, maybe not, I thought, leaving the room to get my tap shoes.

I gave the shoes a quick shine and popped them into my bag. How I loved those little shoes. Because of them I had traveled to Russia, Spain, Paris, and Rio. I had tapped, flamencoed, sambaed, and cariocaed.

Dancing to me was like being set free to whirl out into space, to let go of all my inhibitions and let my body lead me wherever it wanted to go. When I danced, I forgot about George and New Jersey and even my children. I wasn't Mary Louise Temple anymore. I was a shooting star, a sparkling rocket, a flash of light. I hugged my bag with the shoes in them against my chest and did a couple of twirls around the room.

George walked into the room and smiled.

"You're beautiful," he said and kissed me.

"Thank you, sweetheart," I said. "I won't be late. I'm cooking your favorite dinner tonight— salmon and anchovies."

"I may be a little late," he said. "The Alderson Company case is taking longer to prepare for than I thought."

"Tell me again what that case is about," I said, trying to comb the curl out of my hair. I wanted that nice straight look but my hair always rebelled and popped out with a little wiggle whenever it got the chance.

"This woman is suing the company because her husband stepped into an empty elevator shaft in the building they own and was killed."

"That's horrible!" I said. "How do you defend that?"

"It was obviously the fault of the company that built the elevator. The door shouldn't open onto an empty shaft, but it did. It's a complicated case though and it's a lot of work."

He looked preoccupied, worried, and I had a glimpse into the long hours he spent with each case because of his care and perfectionism.

"You'll do a great job," I said. "You always do."

He smiled his thanks and hugged me.

I gave him a quick kiss and went downstairs to wait for Tina and the others.

At nine, right on the dot, Peter's car pulled into our driveway. I like Peter a lot. He makes Tina happy. He had been her husband, Bill's law partner, and he and his wife had been close friends of theirs while Bill was alive. Then Peter and Helen divorced, and a couple of years later, Bill died.

Peter did everything to help Tina adjust to life without Bill. He fell in love with her in the process. Tina just thought of him as a good friend for a long time, but gradually she grew to love him too. They kept talking about getting married, but somehow Tina was always off somewhere dancing instead of arranging the wedding. She was lucky that Peter was such a patient man.

Now that we were going to be in New York for a while, I hoped she would stop putting the wedding off and do it. Tina wanted the reception to be in the Frick Museum in New York, one of my favorite places in the world, as well as hers, because it was so cozy, so much like a home. Knowing Tina, it would be an exquisitely beautiful reception.

I ran outside and hopped in the car where the rest of my Hoofer friends were already ensconced. Somehow all four of us fit in the backseat with plenty of room to sip our coffee and munch on the rolls that Peter had supplied.

"Hey, Weezie," Peter said. "I hear you're going to be a Rockette."

"Is that crazy or what?" I said. "How Tina talked them into letting us dance on that huge stage at Christmastime with all those perfect Rockettes I'll never know."

"Didn't you know?" Peter said with a loving glance at Tina sitting next to him in the front seat. "Tina can do anything."

"Except plan her own wedding," Gini Miller, our documentary filmmaker Hoofer, said, in her usual in-your-face mode.

"Gini," Tina said, her voice low and warning.

"Gini, shut up," Janice Rogers said, using her actress/director voice, instead of her usual gentle one.

"Let's not talk about that right now, Gini," Pat, our peacemaking family therapist Hoofer said, dispelling the threat of a quarrel before we even got out of the driveway.

Peter backed the car into the street and headed for Route 24 that led to Route 78 that would take us through the Lincoln Tunnel and into the city and Rockefeller Center. Peter was an excellent driver and maneuvered his car in and out of the morning traffic with skill.

"So, Tina, what's happening this morning?" Gini asked, choosing a safe subject.

"Well, they were a little vague," Tina said, "but I got the impression that they just wanted to meet us, introduce us to the Rockettes, give us a tour of the theater, and tell us what we will be doing in the show."

"Why are we bringing our tap shoes?" I asked.

"I'm not sure," Tina said, "but I think they want to be sure we can really dance."

"Of course we can dance!" Gini said impatiently. "What do they think we were doing in Rio—directing traffic?"

"Almost getting killed," Pat muttered with a little shudder.

I put my arm around her for a second in a gesture of sympathy. She had been through a terrifying time in Brazil.

Tina reached over the seat and squeezed Pat's

hand. "They knew we were dancing in Rio," she said, "but they want to be sure we can really tap their way. We mostly flung ourselves around doing the samba and the bossa nova in Brazil. It's not the kind of disciplined dancing the Rockettes do."

"Think we can do it?" Janice asked.

"With a lot of work," Tina said. "And I mean long hours of rehearsal."

George will have a fit, I thought, and then, *Tough!* I seemed to be having such ambivalent feelings about him lately. Since I met Mike. I needed to talk to somebody about it. Pat. She's a wonderful therapist. I would talk to her. She always helped. I glanced over at her squeezed into the corner and smiled. She read my mind.

"Will George be OK with long hours away from your wifely duties, Mary Louise?" she asked.

"He'll have to be," I said. "He has no choice."

"There's always a middle way," she said, smiling back at me. "Life isn't just black or white, perfect or not perfect."

"Can we talk?" I said, and my understanding friends chuckled. They all knew how much Pat helped us when we had problems. Every one of us had turned to her in times of crisis and she was always unfailingly wise and insightful.

"Anytime, hon," she said.

Peter emerged from the Lincoln Tunnel, wove his way to Sixth Avenue and Fiftieth Street and let us out in front of Radio City Music Hall.

"Give me a call when you're ready to leave," he said to Tina. "I'll come pick you up."

"We might only be here a short time, Peter," she said. "Don't worry about us. We'll take the train home."

"Call me anyway," he said. "I can usually work something out."

I wished George had such a flexible schedule in his firm as Peter had. George never seemed to be able to "work something out" even though he was the founder of the firm.

We thanked Peter and followed Tina into Radio City.

"May I help you?" the ticket taker said.

"We're the Happy Hoofers," Tina said. "We're looking for Glenna Parsons. We're going to be working with her."

The ticket taker, who looked about fifteen, said, "You're going to be Rockettes?" He tried, but he couldn't hide his disbelief that women our age could possibly be Rockettes. We're only in our early fifties, but to him, we must have seemed ancient.

"You bet we are," Gini said. I love Gini. She always says what the rest of us don't have the nerve to say. "They're begging us to join them. Want to tell Glenna we're here?"

He fumbled with his phone and clicked a button.

"M-m-m-s. Parsons," he said. "They're here."

"Them," he said after a pause. "You know, those Happy Hookers. They're here." People often call us that to tease us, but this boy just made an honest mistake. I think.

Tina gently pried the phone out of his hands.

"Glenna?" she said. "It's Tina. I brought my gang as you requested. We're dying to meet the Rockettes. Where do we go next?"

Tina listened to the answer and then said to us, "She's meeting us on the stage. We ought to be able to find that without any problem."

She handed the phone back to the flustered young man and motioned to the rest of us to follow her into the theater. My first sight of that magnificent foyer brought back the memory of coming to this theater when my children were little. I used to come here when they were in school. In those days, you could see a feature movie, some cowboy short films, a stage show— with the Rockettes of course—and a comedy skit.

I would go into the theater about eleven o'clock and snuggle down in my comfortable seat. I'd pretend I didn't have to go back to my housewifey world. That I could just stay there totally immersed in the feature movie, dancing with them, singing with them, worrying about some incredibly silly problem that of course was solved in ninety minutes. Then I'd stumble out of there around two o'clock and go back home in time to greet my children when they came home from school.

It was heaven. I always came back home refreshed, entertained, calm and ready to cook some more meals, wash some more dishes, pick up stuff all over the house, and drive my children wherever they needed to go after school. I had two boys and a girl and raising them was the best job I ever had and the hardest work.

Two of them are in college now and one in law school, but I wouldn't have traded those years for anything. Radio City was a blessed respite. I still felt that way as I looked at the huge mural on the wall next to the staircase leading up to the balcony showing a man searching for the fountain of youth. Or at least that's what I always thought he was doing.

I followed Tina and the others through the impressive gold doors up the long aisle to the huge stage. Someone once told me the stage was meant to represent the sunrise, with enormous gold arches framing it. Everything in this vast theater produced by Samuel L. Rothafel, which seated six thousand people, was planned to suggest joy and a new day full of promise and fun.

We clambered onto the stage and an attractive woman with dark hair pulled back into a twist, long legs, and a wide smile, hurried out of the wings to greet us.

"Welcome, Hoofers," she said. "I'm Glenna. We are so glad you're going to join us for our Christmas show."

"Hello, Glenna," Tina said and introduced her to each of us.

Glenna looked us over, and we could see her mentally planning makeup, hair arrangements, costume sizes for each one of us. She seemed happiest when she turned her attention to Janice, but we're all used to that. She wouldn't have to do much for Janice because she was so beautiful. Effortlessly beautiful. We'd all hate her if she weren't one of the world's nicest people. Kind, loving, totally unimpressed with her beauty. She just thought of it as something she inherited—like good teeth or nice hair or young skin. Nothing she should be proud of or ashamed of. Useful in the theater. It was just there. And it got us lots of jobs, to be crass about it.

We're all pretty good-looking. Because of the hours we spend dancing, we're slim and in good shape. We also have great legs, but that wasn't really because of dancing. We just inherited them from mothers or grandmothers with smashing gams.

"The Rockettes do their own hair and make-up," Glenna said, "but I thought you might like a little help since you're not used to our system. The girls only wear lipstick, fake eyelashes, and put their hair in a French twist. They're used to it and can do it really fast. Are you OK with a little help?"

We all nodded vigorously, me especially. I couldn't imagine turning into a Rockette with "lipstick, fake eyelashes, and a French twist." My own hair pretty much resisted being pulled back and tied up. Was she kidding?

"That would be great, Glenna," Tina said, speaking for all of us. "What about our costumes?"

"Well, as you know, you're going to do the Santa bit, and the costumes weigh about forty pounds! Think you can dance with that?"

"Forty pounds!" Gini said. "What the heck are they made of—lead?"

Fortunately Glenna laughed. We're never sure how people are going to react to Gini. We're used to her, but not everyone appreciates her comments.

"It has a fat round ball inside it so you'll look like Santa," she said. "But maybe we can work something else out and get lighter costumes for you guys."

"That would be good," Tina said. "Anything you can do to make it easier for us would be wonderful. We want to be like the Rockettes, but I don't think we can ever actually *be* the Rockettes."

"Not to worry," Glenna said. "We'll get you as close to them as we can. Mostly it's rehearse, rehearse, rehearse, and exercise, exercise, exercise. Are you ready for that?"

"You bet," Tina said. "When do you want us to start?"

"Not till tomorrow," Glenna said. "Today, I want you to meet the rest of us Rockettes."

"How many are there?" Pat asked.

"Eighty all together, but we have two separate groups of thirty-six so there are only thirty-six on stage at any one time. With you, there will be forty-one."

Glenna clicked a number on her phone and said, "Send 'em in please, Annie."

The sound of all those tap shoes clickety-clacking down the stairs and onto the stage sounded like an army lining up for inspection. We were soon surrounded by what seemed like thousands of pretty young women, even though there were only eighty. They were smiling and friendly and amazingly lively for that hour of the morning.

"Ladies," Glenna said, "I want you to meet Tina, Gini, Janice, Pat, and Mary Louise. They're the Happy Hoofers. They're going to dance the Santa Claus number with us."

"Lots of luck dancing in jackets that weigh forty pounds," one woman said.

She was one of the taller Rockettes. I knew that you had to be between five feet six inches and five feet ten and a half inches tall to be one of the Rockettes. She must have been about five ten. Her legs looked about five eight by themselves. She had blond hair, highlighted with lighter streaks. She must have been about twenty-five years old, but her face was hard. She didn't smile when she commented on the Santa costumes.

"Knock it off, Marlowe," Glenna said. "I already told them we'd take that fat suit out to make the costumes lighter. Stop trying to scare them."

"If we have to dance in those things, they should have to wear them too," Marlowe said, still unsmiling.

"Audiences are used to seeing us like that,"

Glenna said. "It's a tradition. But our Hoofers here can probably get away without the extra addition."

She looked around at her whole group of Rockettes. "Can I count on you guys to help these Hoofers become temporary Santas?"

Loud shouts of "Sure," and "You bet," and "Of course," made us feel great. I noticed Marlowe didn't join in the general helpful shouts.

"OK," Glenna said. "Let's show them what we'll be doing. Line up and do your stuff." She switched on the music that would be played by a real orchestra for the actual performance.

"When we perform," she continued, "we wear little microphones attached to our shoes to make the tapping louder. You will too. Otherwise people in the back row would miss that great sound."

Microphones on our shoes! I could see this would be unlike any other dancing we had ever done in our lives.

We moved off the stage to watch as the Rockettes lined up and swung into the routine for "Santa Claus Is Coming to Town." They kicked higher than I could ever imagine doing. This was going to take a lot more work than I ever dreamed. But we were going to be Rockettes! Or as close to them as we could manage.

When they finished we jumped to our feet and applauded.

"Think you can do that?" Glenna asked.

"We'll knock ourselves out trying," Tina said.

We all had questions for Glenna.

"When do we start?" Gini said.

"How long will it take us to learn how to dance like they do?" Pat asked.

"What time will we finish rehearsing?" I asked. The memory of George's "Just be sure you're back here in time for dinner," echoed in my mind.

"Do we get a lunch break?" Janice asked. Somehow she always managed to eat all the time and never gain an ounce. I could read her mind, though, and knew she wanted to plan some lunches with her boyfriend, Tom, in her favorite city in the world. I sort of hoped I could sneak in some time with Mike when he wasn't delivering somebody's baby.

"We rehearse every day—not weekends—from ten in the morning until six in the evening," Glenna said. "But we have a lot more routines than you have. We have eight costume changes with every performance and we do five shows a day. You only wear the Santa outfit, and you're all through after that part of the show.

"But you won't spend the whole rehearsal time dancing. We have an hour-long workout of push-ups, leg raises, running in place—lots of things like that. Then we spend the rest of the time practicing the dancing. It's not easy what we do."

"Do you want us to start today?" Tina asked.

"No, today was just a meet-and-greet," Glenna said. "We start tomorrow. Can you get here by ten again?"

"Absolutely," Tina said.

"See you tomorrow then," Glenna said and walked us to the entrance of the theater.

Outside, Tina said, "Want me to call Peter to take us home? Or do you want to spend the day in the city now that we're here?"

We all talked at once telling her we wanted to stay in New York for the day.

"I'm going up to the Frick to start making arrangements for my wedding reception after we finish the Christmas show. Sometime in January maybe," Tina said. "I'll see what's available."

"Think I'll run over to the *Times* and see if Alex is free for lunch and find out what's going on in the city today," Gini said. Alex was a reporter at the *New York Times* and Gini had met him when we danced on a cruise ship in Russia. He had been working in the Moscow office at that time, and the two of them hit it off right away.

Alex loved to travel as much as Gini did. He was impressed with the prize-winning documentary she made about the hurricane in New Orleans. Gini had divorced her husband several years before she met Alex because he wanted her to stay home and clean. That wasn't for our adventurous friend so she left him. Alex was perfect for her. When he heard she was trying to adopt a little girl in India, he volunteered to help her.

The Indian government made it very difficult

for a foreigner to adopt a child in their country. Alex promised to use his resources at the *Times* to find out how she could do that. Gini was obviously in love with Alex, but she was wary of getting married again. For now, they did everything together except say "I do" at the altar. I don't think I've ever seen Gini so happy.

"Guess what?" Janice said. "It's Wednesday! I'm going to get in the TKTS line and go to a matinee this afternoon."

"What are you going to see?" Gini asked.

"Tom's in an off-Broadway play that I want to see. He plays some romantic guy who loses his girlfriend. Or something. I want to see it before it closes. I might decide to stay in town and have dinner with him. I'll call you if I do that, Tina, so you won't wait for me."

"Sounds like fun," Tina said. "Enjoy, Jan."

Pat said she would have lunch with Denise, the woman she lived with in New Jersey, who commuted to her job at a public relations firm in New York.

"I don't often get to see Denise during the week because she's in the city and I'm home counseling clients," she said. "This will be a special treat for us." She clicked on her phone to make the call.

"What about you, Weezie?" Tina said. "Want to come to the Frick with me? I know you love that museum."

"No, thanks, Tina," I said. "I want to eat in some restaurant by the water."

I really wanted to have lunch with Mike, but I didn't mention it to my friends. It didn't seem right to see him again, but I knew I would call him. I loved talking to him and I wanted to tell him about the Music Hall.

"Bye then, everyone," Tina said. "Let's meet here around five and Peter will take us home."

"See ya," Gini said, heading toward the *Times* building.

When they had all scattered in different directions, I called Mike.

"Hey, love," he said. "When's your baby due?"

I laughed. He always makes me laugh. He never starts a conversation asking me why I didn't do something I was supposed to do.

"Hi, Mike," I said. "I'm in New York. Any chance you've got a free minute or two to meet me for lunch or a walk or something?"

"I have more than a minute or two," he said, his voice reflecting his pleasure in hearing mine. "Let's meet at The Boathouse restaurant in the park for lunch." How did he know I wanted to eat by the water? The same way he always guessed what I really wanted to do.

"Sounds lovely," I said. "When?"

"Immediately," he said. "Grab a cab and meet me there as soon as you can. I can't wait to see you."

I found a cab right away and it took me through Central Park to the entrance of The Boathouse restaurant with tables on the veranda outside that looked out on the water and people paddling rowboats away from the shore. It was a beautiful fall day, and the trees were in full glory, reaching their colorful leaves toward the sun.

Mike was already there when my cab pulled up. He scooped me out of my seat, paid the driver, and held me tight until we were seated by the railing next to the pond. The Boathouse had formerly fulfilled the function suggested by its name, but now its gracious proportions were the home of a popular restaurant.

"Don't you have any babies to deliver or new mothers to advise or something medical you're supposed to be doing?" I said when we were sitting across from each other, separated only by a white linen tablecloth and a small vase of yellow chrysanthemums.

"Nobody is even due today," he said. "Why haven't you called me, Mary Louise?"

"Oh, Mike, you know why," I said.

"I know why, but I don't accept it," he said. "You know I love you. I'll always love you. And if you won't leave George, I still want to see you because you love me, too, even if you won't admit it. You told me you loved me in Spain."

"Mike," I said, "try to understand. George and I have been married for thirty years. I can't throw those years away just like that. And it would hurt my children if I left him."

"They're grown. Or almost grown," he said. "They would learn to accept it."

"Don't ask me to leave him, Mike," I said. "Please don't. It's unfair of me to keep seeing you like this when I know I'm not going to leave George, but I can't help it. I love being with you, talking to you. You make me laugh. You make me feel good about myself. George has forgotten how to do that."

"For now, I'll settle for a lunch whenever you're in New York," he said.

I smiled.

"What's funny?" he asked.

"Well, the truth is, I'm going to be in New York every day until January," I said. "We're dancing with the Rockettes in their Christmas show."

He grabbed my hand. "You're kidding," he said, obviously delighted. "We can have lunch every day."

"What if some woman decides to have her baby in the middle of the day?" I asked.

"She'll just have to wait," he said. I knew he was kidding. He was the most caring, conscientious doctor I had ever met. He truly cherished the women who came to him to have their babies.

"I don't even know if they're going to give us time to eat a real lunch,"

I said. "We're going to be rehearsing and exercising and Rocketting for hours every day."

"Just the fact that you're in the city every day," he said, "means that we can have some time together, babies and rehearsal times permitting."

The waiter hovered. "Want a drink?" Mike asked me.

"Maybe a glass of white wine," I said.

"Let's make it a Kir Royale," he said, remembering my favorite drink of champagne and crème de cassis.

I hesitated. Oh, why not? "Sure," I said. I didn't have to dance or drive.

"How was Rio?" he asked when the waiter went off to get our drinks.

"Except for a murder or three it was beautiful," I said. "Have you ever been there? I forget."

"My wife and I went there on our honeymoon," he said. "We stayed at the Copacabana. Gorgeous hotel."

"That's where we were," I said. "And it's still gorgeous."

The waiter brought our drinks and asked if we had decided on lunch.

"What's good here, Mike?" I asked.

"Everything," he said. "Why don't you get an omelet or their quiche, which is excellent, or a salad? They have a great lobster salad here."

"I love lobster," I said. "That's what I'll have."

Mike raised his glass. "Here's to lunch with you every day of my life when I'm not delivering a baby," he said.

I clinked my glass against his and took a sip. It was lovely.

My phone vibrated. I usually don't answer my phone when I'm with another person. I think it's rude. But something made me answer this call.

"Mary Louise?" Tina said. "You won't believe this, but Glenna—you know, the Rockette we met this morning—she's dead."

"What do you mean she's dead?" I said. "What happened to her?"

"They found her under the stage, mangled in the machinery."

"My God," I said. "What are we supposed to do now?"

"The woman who called me—remember Marlowe, one of the Rockettes—said we have to return to the theater immediately. The police are there and the captain wants to talk to all of us."

"How soon?"

"As soon as you can get back here. Where are you?"

"At The Boathouse," I said.

"With Mike?" she asked. Tina knows everything.

"As a matter of fact—" I started to say.

"Never mind," she said. "Just get back here as soon as you can."

"What's the matter?" Mike asked when I put my phone back in my purse.

"You won't believe this," I said. "But one of the Rockettes—the one we met this morning—is dead."

"You guys have got to stop performing," he said. "She'd probably still be alive if you hadn't shown up."

"It's not funny, Mike," I said.

"I know, honey," he said. "I didn't mean to make fun of this. Come on, I'll take you back to the theater."

He took a sip of the Kir Royale, left money on the table, and led me out to the street where there were cabs waiting.

Acknowledgments

Once again, I want to thank Michaela Hamilton for her superb editing of this book and all the books in the Happy Hoofer series. She has been unfailingly supportive and enthusiastic as I took my dancers through four countries and countless murders. And again, I'm grateful to everyone at Kensington Publishing Corp. for making my books so readable and attractive.